HIND POCKET BOOKS

VAASTU FOR HEALTH, WEALTH AND HAPPINESS

An alumni of Modern School and St.Stephens College, Delhi, Mr. Rakesh Chawla feels he was destined to be a Vaastu proponent. It was during his tenure with Philips India that he was introduced to Vaastu Shastra in 1988. Since the past 20+ years, he has been refining and redefining the subject to make it easy to follow for the lay reader.

Vaastu For Health, Wealth and Happiness

Rakesh Chawla

HIND POCKET BOOKS
An imprint of Penguin Random House

HIND POCKET BOOKS

USA | Canada | UK | Ireland | Australia
New Zealand | India | South Africa | China | Singapore

Hind Pocket Books is part of the Penguin Random House group of companies whose addresses can be found at global.penguinrandomhouse.com

Published by Penguin Random House India Pvt. Ltd
4th Floor, Capital Tower 1, MG Road,
Gurugram 122 002, Haryana, India

Penguin
Random House
India

First published in Hind Pocket Books by Penguin Random House India 2019
This edition published in 2022

10 9 8 7 6 5 4 3 2

The views and opinions expressed in this book are the author's own and the facts are as reported by him which have been verified to the extent possible, and the publishers are not in any way liable for the same.

ISBN 9789353493479

Printed at Repro India Limited

www.penguin.co.in

MIX
Paper from responsible sources
FSC® C047271
FSC www.fsc.org

Contents

Praise for Raakesh Chawla

Jayant Kapur
CEO Bacardi Martini India Ltd.

"My first contact with Raakesh Chawla was during a period when there was significant pressure on me, both at home and at business. He came with a very strong recommendation from a friend.

Raakesh comes across as a very unassuming person but is a clear thinker. His ability to get to the root cause of the issue is phenomenal. He seems to be able to almost visualize the processes and interactions taking place in any environment and comes up with solutions that are most practical.

In this book you will experience not only Raakesh's deep understanding of the principles of Vaastu but also its application in different situations and relationships. There is an easy flow to the book which is very reminiscent of Raakesh's personality. In an extremely uncomplicated way he gains the reader's appreciation of Vaastu. I personally started off as a sceptic but now am a keen believer of Vaastu. I am sure after reading this book you will experience a similar commitment and appreciation of Vaastu."

Jairam Ramesh
Secretary, Congress Party

"Vaastu is ancient India's distinctive contribution to the practice of architecture. Till now, it was wrapped up in a whole lot of esoteric mumbo-jumbo. We had all heard of it. Most of us laughed it away as superstitious nonsense. Those who believed in it tended to be dismissed as cranks or as prisoners of non-scientific thinking.

Not any longer. Raakesh Chawla demolishes the myth of Vaastu lacking in substance. In easy-to-read language and with apt illustrations, he unravels the myriad mysteries of Vaastu and explains its multifarious facets in meticulous detail. Vaastu is a comprehensive philosophy of living and is an integral part of our Vedic legacy. It is a menu for peace and prosperity. Raakesh reinterprets this hoary recipe for modern-day applications.

This is a book that will educate and enlighten you. It will appeal not only to the initiated but more importantly to the larger group of the curious and the sceptics. He deserves kudos for this venture. I was fascinated by this treatise. Not converted but definitely more sympathetic to his cause."

Sanjiv Keshava
Divisional CEO-ITC
Lifestyle Retail Business Division

"I met Raakesh three years ago and took an instant liking to him. His warmth, honesty, simplicity and genuineness drew me like a magnet. Raakesh has a very simplistic way of looking at life and continually strives to make it as less complex as possible. His interpretations of the elements and his deciphering of complicated rituals and societal laws are simple, earthy and practical. His new book delves into the fundamentals of life forms, the elements of earth, water, space and time.

He interprets energy as the driving force of all life. Refreshingly, he explains energy as an omnipresent vibration and not derived through ritualistic and supernatural forms. Raakesh provides a very practical approach to Vaastu, beginning at the fundamentals and leads us on to simplistic and uncomplicated ways to trap these energies first within ourselves, then in our environment. These energies create harmony, peace and calm within us followed by all others around us.

You can be rest assured that you will not have to break walls and displace all your favourites to attain peace. The aim is to achieve the same results with the use of simple remedial measures that he suggests with great precision."

Shivraj V. Patil
Former Speaker of Lok Sabha

"This book explains that Vaastu is scientific and convincing. It dispels the doubts and strikes at the root of the theory of superstition behind Vaastu Shastra. The book is written in a lucid and easy-to-understand language which will help the reader to grasp what the author wants to convey. It will be most useful to those who want to build houses, shops or industrial structures. There are one or two statements in the book with which I may not agree. All the same, I found it very enjoyable to read, and I am sure, it would be useful to many.

I congratulate the author for bringing out this book, and wish him all the best."

Introduction

Many times I have been asked if Vaastu really works? And why this sudden awareness in Vaastu with everyone joining the bandwagon?

Well, Vaastu isn't nuclear science or space technology that a lay person cannot understand. It is a subject linking man with nature that is both outside and within. Its principles are easy to follow. The resurgence of Vaastu has many theories behind it. Is it global competition that forces the corporate biggies to follow anything which offers a cutting edge or is it the placement of Neptune that spirituality is suddenly in and a lot of esoteric concepts are being talked about. I personally feel it is the availability of information in the print and electronic media (including the internet) plus thousands of books which have flooded the market enabling free and easy access to information as the main cause. Don't forget that a few years ago the knowledge of this subject was confined to a learned few and handed down only by word of mouth.

It is interesting to note that Vaastu has come about at a time when a majority of the construction around the world is not Vaastu friendly. Such a scenario could easily suggest large scale demolition and reconstruction in accordance with the scriptures, which is not practical. Therefore, it is strongly recommended to follow remedial methods and harness the elements without making major structural changes.

But some people get carried away by myths that they have probably come across. East is the direction of inspiration, North of wealth, West is equated with retirement as the sun sets in that direction and South is also said to be the direction of Yama or the lord of death. A lot of companies have either shifted their entrances from South to North or have moved places. Some have even brought down their buildings because they were facing South or death. It is an irrational advice that they follow because if South is death then which direction offers immortality?

Some businessmen undertake major structural changes in their offices and spend large sums of money in renovations simply after reading a few books or articles on Vaastu. The result is most of them are unhappy. Do you know why? They forget that most books only speak of the ideal situation as mentioned in the ancient scriptures and not the practical application of knowledge contained therein. Answer this question honestly: When you fall sick do you read a book on medicine and start treating yourself or do you consult a doctor? Then how come after reading a book or two you start treating your office. Please don't follow quick fix solutions as they can be very damaging. The concept of Vaastu is a guide for linking man with nature which is both outside as well as within and the subject matter of this book is an effort to do the same.

THE THEORY & PHILOSOPHY OF VAASTU

Chapter One

Vaastu — An Introduction

What is Vaastu?

The caveman thought of his abode as his safe haven when he returned after a day's hunting. It was a place of rest, a place of shelter and comfort. Man has taken centuries to evolve, but as he has evolved, so has something evolved with him — his way of making a home for himself. He has come a long way from his dwelling in the caves. But his homing instinct is still with him, as he builds his bungalows, villas, country-houses, flats, apartments, factories or shops. An enormous range of homes that have been built, in different parts of the world — the igloo of the Eskimo, the wigwam of the Red Indian, the *shikara* of the Kashmiri — are all instances of man's basic need to have a home. The whole science of architecture has developed because of this instinct of man.

India has an exceptionally rich heritage of architecture. Even before the Aryans came to India, the people — named *dasyus* by the invading Aryans — lived in constructed houses. The Rigveda (i, 103, 3) refers to Indra as the destroyer of *dasih purah,* the dwellings of the *dasyus.* Even if one were to argue that *'purah'* does not mean much more than rough hamlets, at least they were man-made constructions — not just natural caves.

These constructions were based on certain principles keeping in mind the flow of energy through the home. The Universe is full of beneficial energies that we must learn to harness as well as to keep in balance for our well-being. This life force around us is called Vaastu.

The history of Vaastu

Vaastu in ancient times was confined to architects (*sthapathis*) and handed down by word of mouth or through handwritten monographs. It was treated as the science for the construction of temples and royal palaces. The principles of construction, architecture and sculpture have been incorporated in this science.

Epics like the *Bruhatsamhita, Vishnu Dharmottara Purana, Viswakarma Vaastu Shastra, Samarangana Sutra Dharana* and *Aparajita Prutchcha,* have also been responsible for Vaastu taking its shape as a science.

The first official treatise on Vaastu, the *Kasyapa Silpa,* has been attributed to sage Kasyapa. In the treatise *Agama*

Shastra, which explains the science of temples, Vaastu is considered the basis for any type of construction. Excavations at Harappa and Mohenjodaro have also shown the influence of Vaastu on the Indus Valley civilisation.

During the Vedic period, there developed a body of architectural ideas which came to be known as Vaastu Shastra. These ideas were embodied in the Vedas, the Puranas, the *Grhyasutras,* and several later works like the Manasara.

The epics describe cities, multi-storeyed buildings, arches, balconies and other forms of architecture. In the Ramayana, the city of Ayodhya had high walls, assembly halls, and high-steepled houses. Lanka was a marvel of decorative palaces and tall structures. The Mahabharata provides a short but graphic description of cities like Indraprastha, Dwaraka, Mithila, and the assembly-halls of gods.

Houses in ancient India could not be constructed and used just anyhow. There were certain norms and procedures regarding them, which even the royalty followed. These are all compiled in the Vaastu Shastra and cover all aspects of the science of building. The Vaastu Shastra (treatise) views the physical environment as an expression of the cosmic spirit. A building in essence is a re-creation of the cosmos. The direction of the building, the relationship between the building and its environment, the soil type of the land and the shape of the plot all affects the energies that flow through the building. The flow of energy in turn affects those who live in these buildings.

Vaastu — a magic?

When you believe in Vaastu life becomes simpler/easier. Time and again I have been asked by my readers and clients, "Is Vaastu really a science?" Or "Why this sudden awareness and interest in Vaastu? How come it is the 'in' thing today, is it just a fad or is it here to stay?" The first mention of Vaastu is in the Rigveda, and subsequently one finds its reference in the holy epics of the Ramayana (Sri Valmiki's Ashram) and Mahabharata (Dwaraka), an era when philosophy was a way of life. The questioning and reasoning behind philosophical thoughts or ideas eventually led to the beginning of this science as we understand it today. Areas where logical explanation has not yet been possible, fall in the realm of mysticism. I personally think Vaastu can best be described as a 'mystic science' that governs the energies of the human existence. Just as medical science has explored and explained various aspects of the human body while the existence of the soul remains a mystery, so the principles of Vaastu are the principles of health of the body; while the spirit of Vaastu still remains a mystery.

Considered an integral part of the Indian home, Vaastu's significance stems from much more than the placing of a window. It works on the basic premise that the earth or soil is actually alive, and that all living or organic creatures emerge directly from it. This life force within the earth is called Vaastu, and all objects placed on it share this life force. The earth, therefore, works as both substance and support. Vaastu is also explained as the living space — *Vaastu* meaning 'to live' or 'to reside'.

The principal parameters which govern Vaastu diktats have evolved around natural phenomena; however, any explanation about its varying intensity on different individuals remains a mystery. The intensity of the effect depends on one's beliefs. And the right knowledge contributes greatly in shaping one's beliefs. Therefore, *an elemental understanding of Vaastu is essential before laying your belief system on it.*

The mysticism prevails, otherwise we could have had set formulas for becoming Presidents, Prime Ministers, actors, businessmen or whatever we wanted and the excitement or thrill would not have existed if we could just build a magical structure to fulfill all our fantasies and dreams. The renewed interest in Vaastu over the past few years is also thought provoking. Is it liberalisation and global competition that has led to its revival; or is it the dawning of the spiritual era to which the world has suddenly awakened and esoteric concepts like Reiki and

Pranic Healing have also emerged; or is it the placement of the planet Neptune that has aroused spirituality.

How Vaastu works

Whether or not you believe in Vaastu, it affects your well-being. Space, time and energy are traditionally perceived as existing in their free, unlimited state. Vaastu believes that these three elements can be disciplined by applying rhythm and order (in other words, science) to the way we live, move, and use time.

The word 'Vaastu' is derived from the root Vas which means to live or to reside. Vaastu therefore deals with the art of living in accordance with a holistic view of life where man is deeply connected with the universe and the energy of the elements. Vaastu blends the psychological with the philosophical to harness the energy waves to our benefit. The practice of Vaastu helps us to create a harmonious space.

We exist because of the five universal elements

Our existence on this planet can originally be attributed to a simple phenomenon called the natural cycle. According to this cycle, water evaporates due to solar heat and is transformed into clouds. These clouds give way to rain (lightning and thunder), and rain water is recycled to

The five universal elements.

support vegetation as well as maintain the water balance on earth. You will see that there are five basic components of the nature cycle: water or rain, heat or evaporation, clouds or air, thunder or space, and the earth, are none other than the five universal elements of water, fire, air, space and earth. These are the very attributes of any physical manifestation which can be perceived by our sense organs of taste, sight, touch, sound and smell. Our tools of perception have remained the same throughout the evolution of mankind.

It has been observed that an imbalance of the five elements in the natural cycle can create calamities like earthquakes, volcanoes, typhoons, tornadoes, floods or drought. Similarly on a micro scale when it comes to an individual or a family, such an imbalance can cause physical, mental or emotional upheavals.

The origin of the five universal elements is from *Bhagvan.* Our universe is Bhagvan. *Bh* represents *Bhoomi, a* represents *Agni, g* represents *Gagan, va* represents *Vayu* and *n* represents *Neer.* Our sense organs also emerged from *Bhagvan* which are linked to our mind *(Mann)* through the fabric of life (*Prana*). These universal elements reside in specific directions such as *Bhoomi* (Earth) in the South-west, *Agni* (Fire) in the South-east, *Gagan* (Space) in the Centre, *Vayu (*Air) in the North-west and *Neer* (Water) in the North-east. Therefore, one is advised not to tamper with the embodiment of the elements, rather enhance your activities in conjunction with the inert nature of the elements.

All human beings are bogged down by the five core issues

Interestingly we also have five core issues (Maslow's theory) around which life revolves, these are **security and stability in life** (Earth/South-west). **Progress** which could mean either a growing family or a burgeoning business (Water/North-east). **Health, physical or professional** (Fire/South-east). **Relationships** at home or place of work *(*Air/North-west) and the urge to **communicate** with one's inner self as well as with others (Space/Centre). Any other issue is either a combination or derivation of these core issues.

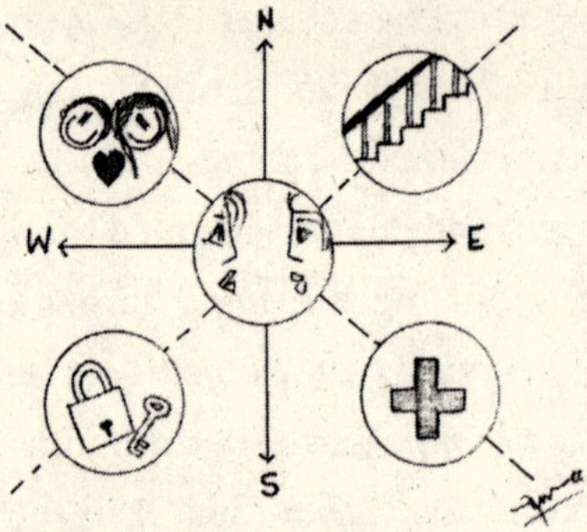

Best directions for core issues.

When you face multiple problems it is not advisable to tackle all the issues simultaneously as this would lead to dissipation of energy and the results will not be to your satisfaction. Hence, it is very important to first identify the core issue and then take remedial action. Try this exercise. Think about yourself and what is bothering you the most. Translate that to its element/direction and try to locate the obstacle. Once the obstacle has been identified, removing it is not difficult.

For easy flow of energy, use cardinal directions

Since Vaastu is a science of directions and utilising them to the optimum is important, we must first know how to find them with the use of a compass. There are two types of compasses available in the market — Floating Disc and Pivotal Needle. The Floating Disc compass has a rotating disc with markings of East, West, North and South on it. To determine the directions inside a house all you need to do is place the compass at the centre and the pointers will indicate all the directions simultaneously. While using the Pivotal Needle compass you again have to place it near the centre and wait for the needle to stop oscillating, the coloured tip of the needle always points towards the North. You need to align the North marked N on the dial directly below the needle and the other three directions get positioned by gradually moving the body of the compass. The pointer of the directions is the same inside or outside any structure. A slight variation may occur due to beams and columns which is negligible. Remember when we say the building faces East, it means the main gate or entrance door opens towards the East while you face West on entering.

Cardinal directions have a great impact on the life of human beings. Tradition has granted each direction a unique, mystic meaning. Therefore, to set up a perfect North-South, East-West axis on the site is a very important aspect of design. After plotting the North-South-East-West axis, the plot or Vaastu should be set out into modules. This procedure is known as *pada vinyasa*.

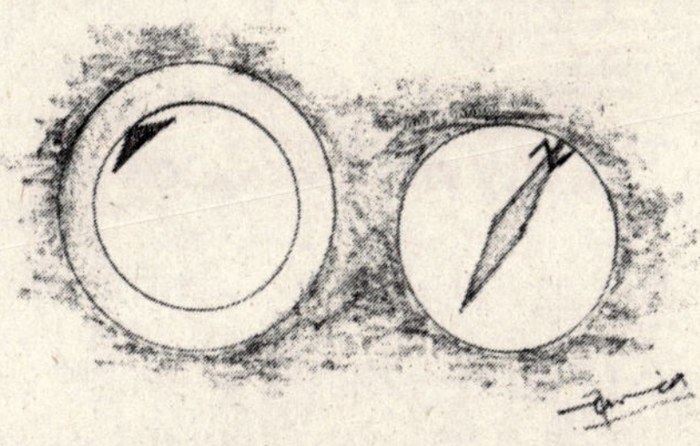

a) The Floating Disc compass.
b) The Pivotal Needle compass.

Brahmasthana

This is the centre of the plot and the balance in life comes from it. In the design it is important to create a centre for the building from which it grows into the total form. This growth out of the centre is comparable to the 'experience of centre', where creative action is brought out from. For meaningful action, the weight and energy of the form is anchored in the centre.

The *brahma pada* or *veethi*

This is the central area of the total form which includes the central point. In the process of design the *brahma pada* is considered to have very high concentration of energy (of the total form). Therefore, traditionally it was either opened out as the courtyard or made into a central hall for a collective gathering.

The *deivika pada* or *veethi*

This is the first concentric space around the central *brahma pada.* In this space, the energies are considered to be fairly high and so the allocation of passages and rooms for collective rather than individual use, such as dining and family rooms are recommended here.

The *manusha pada* or *veethi*

This is the second concentric space. It is considered to contain energy which is fairly comfortable for human activity and, therefore, all activity rooms such as kitchen, bedrooms, study areas, puja and rooms for individual use may be placed in this part of the layout.

The *paisaacha pada* or *veethi*

The final concentric space which can contain the storage areas, outer verandah, external walls, outer walkways and activity areas such as bedrooms and workrooms. In general, *manusha* and *paisaacha* may be considered together for all special activity areas.

For everlasting happiness, worship Vaastudeva/Purusha

In the Mahabharata, when the Pandavas had burnt down the Khandava forest, they had spared the life of a *danava* named Maya who was the architect of the *danavas.* As a mark of gratitude, Maya constructed for them a wonderful palace. It contained buildings with steeples as high as mountain-peaks, gold-latticed windows, stairs with easy slopes, and shining white walls. It was there that the Pandavas held their *rajasuya yajna* and hosted the prominent *ksatriyas* who came to attend it.

But Yudhisthira, the eldest of the Pandavas, did not enter it without the due ceremonies. The Sabhaparvan of the Mahabharata clearly mentions that Yudhisthira held a feast for ten thousand *brahmins* with fruits and roots, pork and venison, rice pudding mixed with clarified butter and honey. He garlanded them and presented them with valuable garments and numerous cows. To the accompaniment of music and songs Yudhisthira worshipped the gods and only then did he enter the palace. For a whole week afterwards, Yudhisthira arranged programmes of sports and music to entertain the kings and sages who had gathered at his palace.

Even in epic times, there was indeed a ritual to be performed when entering a newly constructed building, built in this case for both residential and administrative purposes.

In the Indian way of life, a man's life is divided into four stages (*asramas*): *brahmacarya, grahasthya, vanaprastha* and *sannyasa*. Just as there are guidelines regarding the stages of *brahmacarya, vanaprastha* and *sannyasa,* there are guidelines regarding the stage of *grahasthya*. The *Grhyasutras,* for example, tell us how everyday as well as ceremonial activities should be conducted by a *grahasthya* or householder. The Puranas too give advice on how to be a good householder.

विभागयीलः सततम क्षमायुतो दयालुः
ग्टहस्यस्तु समारयारते न ग्टहेण ग्टही भवेत॥

vibhagasilah satatam ksamayukto dayaluh
grhsthastu samakhyato na grhena grhi bhavet.
Padmapurana svargakhandam 26/24

Just having a house does not make one a good householder. A good householder is one who has judgement, mercy and kindness.

It is not just *brahmacarya, vanaprastha* and *sannyasa* that are conceived of as spiritual experiences for humankind. *Grahasthya* too is a spiritual experience, an important part of the overall upliftment of human existence.

It is only logical that the *grha,* such a very important element of the *grahasthya* stage, should be entered with utmost respect.

The construction (*nirmana*) of and entry (*pravesa*) into houses are called *salakarma* in the *Grhyasutras.*

Here are some of the guidelines regarding them:

- The most suitable months for constructing houses are *Vaisakha* (April-May), *Asada* (June-July), *Sravana* (July-August), *Kartika* (October-November) and *Falguna* (February-March). It is auspicious to start construction in the lunar fortnight (*Sukla paksa*) and inauspicious in the dark fortnight (*Krsna paksa*).
- It is also considered auspicious to start construction on any day other than a Tuesday and Saturday.

- The prescription (*vidhi*) is to start construction only on an auspicious day (*subhadina*), and only after worshipping Vaastudeva and other gods.
- After the house has been constructed, the *Grhapravesa* ceremony has to be performed. This is preferred when the sun is in the northern hemisphere, that is, between 22 June and 22 December. It is to be done *only* on a day found to be *subha* or auspicious. It is auspicious in the following *lagunas: Kanya* (Virgo), *kumbha* (Aquarius), *vrsa* (Taurus), *vrscika* (Scorpio), *simha* (Leo) and *mithun* (Gemini) and on the following days of the week: Monday, Wednesday, Thursday and Friday.
- In the *Grhapravesa* ceremony, the householder has to enter the new house with his wife, family and other relations and friends.

He should do so in the morning, carrying some rice with him. His wife, too, must enter at the same time, carrying a pot of water at her waist or on her shoulder.

According to the Yajurveda, the wife should walk ahead of the husband, whereas according to the Samaveda she should walk by his side. According to the Rigveda, the householder has to make his entry not only with his wife but his eldest son as well. On entering the house, the householder has to do the following *pujas: Vaastupuja* and associated *pujas* — *Nandimukha sraddha* and *havan.*

The basic Vaastu Purusha Mandala.

He has to address what is known as the *Vaastudeva, Vastispati, Vaastu Purusha, Vaastupala,* or *Vaasturajan* who is the deity presiding over the house, and is conceived of as bright, adorned with a gold necklace, crown and sacred thread. He carries the replica of the earth in one hand, and makes the *mudra* (gesture) of *varabhaya* (assurance and reward) in the other. Apart from the occasion of *Grhapravesa*, he has to be worshipped on the occasion of *sraddha* performances and the *samkranti* of the month of *Pausa* (December-January).

The prayer to him is along the following lines:

You are the owner of this site that we have come to live in. Please be acquainted with us, accept our offerings, and regard us as members of your own family. Give us your blessings. Protect us from danger and sorrow, and help us to live in peace and amity among ourselves.

For faster results combine Vaastu and Astrology

Vaastu and astrology have both originated from the Vedas and are inter-dependent. In fact, both are derived from each other and complement each other as well. Vaastu Shastra, depends on astrology to find out *muhurta* (auspicious moments). An astrologer, while performing *yagnas*, must depend on Vaastu for the location. While both the sciences are independent and complete in themselves, a joint study helps in understanding the environment better.

Is Vaastu connected to astrology? Although these are two independent sciences they do share a common zone as do numerology and palmistry. The knowledge of allied sciences is incorporated to determine the auspicious time or date for initiating any construction, *Bhoomi Pujan, Grhapravesa* and in some cases to determine the most suitable city or area for a person to live in, based upon his name and date of birth. Some traditional families, especially in Southern India, continue to follow these principles, passing on the knowledge from one generation to the next.

In astrology there are two planets, Rahu and Ketu, referred to as the shadows of the sun and moon. They are also known as the dragon's head and tail. In either connotation they are nodal points, incomplete in themselves and always searching for communion. In numerology these planets or shadows are represented by the numbers 4 and 7 respectively. People born under these numbers always have a spiritual quest, which they nurture when their inward journey begins. In Vaastu, these planets have been assigned the South-west and the North-east directions. The axis connecting these two is of vital importance for preparing the architectural layout of any building and any impeachment of Vaastu law for these two quadrants yields the maximum discomfort to the occupant. To stay clear of their malefic effect, you must ensure that no shadow ever falls on your main door, dining table, cooking vessels and your bed as it could have undesirable consequences. Vaastu recommends installing of an extra light to nullify their effect.

APPLICATIONS OF VAASTU

Chapter Two

Ground Rules

Applying the rules of Vaastu to our lives

For constructing a house, the principles of Vaastu are based upon a uniform pattern and follow certain basic rules of direction. It is believed that a deviation from the guidelines might have an adverse effect on those living there.

Three principles of design have been put forth, which cover the entire field of design, whether it is a building, a craft item or an article of daily use.

Bhogadyam: The designed product must be useful and lend itself to easy application.

Sukha darsham: The designed product must be aesthetically pleasing. This principle covers the exterior of a building as well as the interior.

Ramya: The designed product must be capable of evoking a feeling of well-being and contentment.

In Vaastu there are multiple ways in which the designer and occupant can create a space for experience. If the space has a specific activity, then gathering all the energies in a single centre proves to be very powerful.

Though the science of Vaastu follows generic rules, there are certain specific principles that Vaastu practitioners believe in, viz.:

- The rooms in the eastern and northern part of the house must have a smaller carpet area than those located in the western and southern parts. This principle is followed due to the belief that the eastern parts of the house are sensitive to heavy loads. There must be an equal distribution of heavy and light rooms in the house for a free flow of positive energy.
- The North-eastern part of the house is also very sensitive, and care must be taken to see that no heavy object is placed in that part of the house. Heavy objects like cabinets and refrigerators must be arranged in the southern or western direction. These principles are followed to maintain a sense of balance, and are universally applicable.

For stress-free living, understand your environment

Vaastu is a subject that links man with nature. The principles of Vaastu are easy to follow at the beginning of any construction. Since all directions are the embodiment of a universal element it is recommended to carry out an activity in a manner that harmonizes with the inert nature of the element.

According to the law of physics every action has an equal and opposite reaction. Our action is not only the physical act that we perform but also what we say and most importantly what we think. Very often we think one thing but speak something else and do something totally different. When our action is at three different tangents what kind of result can we expect? Today, a lot of people follow Vaastu as non-believers and when the results are not satisfactory, they criticise it. To attain the most favourable results, it is recommended to follow this subject willingly and wholeheartedly.

Live in harmony with nature.

Vaastu does not prescribe giving up material pursuits and following the path of spirituality. It emphasises understanding yourself and your surroundings. It thus guides you towards a path on which your self-healing mechanism always remains active and obstacles are easily overcome. Remember, all human beings are self-healers. We were created in perfect health and harmony and our inner voice constantly guides us towards the same, but the noise of the world outside consistently pulls us away from health and harmony. The adjustments we make in our day to day living are referred to by some as destiny. Actually we have these experiences so that we realise who we really are.

According to the Quantum theory, when an atom is broken to its millionth part it appears to be a vibration wherein conjugates of solids have a denser vibration than liquids and gases. What does Quantum theory have in common with Vaastu? Vaastu gets its rationality from the Q theory. After all, the vibration of a place determines your well-being since you are constantly exchanging energies with the objects and people in your surroundings. Vaastu stimulates good vibrations ensuring peace of mind. How does this happen? Every object has a specific vibration. When the collective vibration of a room or house are in tandem with your body, you feel happy, otherwise you shall always be restless in that area. But you need not get upset when you discover that your house/office is not Vaastu perfect and please do not make any structural changes as they are equivalent to surgery on the human body, which is undertaken only as a last resort. Very often we can overcome our illness with medication, change in diet and lifestyle. Likewise, reorientation of furniture and the basic layout can prove to be extremely helpful as it changes the existing vibration and you begin to vibe well at home, and, you become a happier person.

Who says Vaastu is only for the rich?

The lifestyle of the rich and famous actually has no room for Vaastu because their westernised outlook does not recognise this subject. They resort to it only when in deep trouble and soon realise its potential and start following it religiously. On the other hand, an average person can derive the maximum benefit from this science because of his outlook and faith in mystic concepts. It has been observed that it is easy for any esoteric concept to gain popularity with the elite because they are far more insecure and scared of any kind of loss. The principles of Vaastu are the same for a flat or a farmhouse as the sun's trajectory shall always be East-West and the magnetic axis remains North-South. The social strata has no relevance in the cosmic design. Some people are scared to follow Vaastu as it might entail structural changes which are not affordable. This is not true because surgery (Structural Change) is undertaken as a last resort. Generally remedial measures are more than sufficient.

Vaastu is for all human beings, not just the rich.

Vaastu defects can deter progress

Vaastu defects can be classified into different categories such as primary defect, secondary defect and contributory defect. These are supported by a compensating factor. A primary defect relates directly to the problem experienced by those dwelling in the building and is the main reason for its manifestation. A secondary defect is one which lies in the opposite sector or quadrant and adds to the negativity of a primary defect, making it more potent. A contributory defect has a bearing on both. While the compensating factors are considered a divine grace, the absence of these can cause inmates to be miserable. Thus when you equate two houses which are say South facing, please keep in mind all the factors that can have a bearing on the experience of the inmates. We cannot generalise that all South facing properties are redundant and all East facing will be prosperous. The analysis should be in totality, not in isolation of any single factor.

While purchasing a property one must not only evaluate the Vaastu friendliness of the building but must also verify the genuineness of the proposals in terms of legalities and adherence of bye-laws of the state. If a building does not conform to the bye-laws, it has a built-in primary defect, which can easily become magnified by a secondary or contributory defect, such as wrong placement of the kitchen, master bedroom, uneven floor levels etc., causing many discomforts to the occupants in the years to come.

28

Harness positive energies for good health

The principles of Vaastu help in achieving harmony between external and internal energies. The external energies are in the form of heat, light, sound and so on, which we constantly receive from our surroundings. The internal energies are commonly routed through our diet, sleeping habits and above all our mind or thought processes. A dissonance in internal energies reflects on our physical health, whereas dissonance in external energies might create mental unrest.

When the internal and external energies are balanced, health, wealth and happiness unfolds. For example, when we sleep with our head towards the North, we may experience discomfort in the form of low or high blood pressure, insomnia or a high level of cholesterol. This is because our head is considered the North (end) of the body, and sleeping with our head towards the North creates repulsion between two similar poles according to the theory of magnetism. The effect can be reduced or rectified by reversing the head position to the South.

The layout of the house and the orientation of furniture play a vital role in receiving positive natural energies like sunlight, air, electromagnetic currents and so on which can easily be incorporated especially by those who are constructing a new house. However, people already residing in a house (owned or rented) should not undertake any structural changes simply after reading a book or an article. Look for easy solutions. I am repeating time and again, do not undertake structural changes because many simple solutions are available now. Remember, Vaastu is the linking of man with nature both from the outside and from within.

Chapter Three

Plot and Structure

Which plot is lucky?

How to ascertain whether a plot will be lucky? First of all, to own a plot in a big city is lucky enough. This needs to be supported by building a structure in accordance with Vaastu to ensure prosperity and harmony. While selecting a plot you need to look at the soil colour, any existing vegetation and surrounding structures, as each of these plays an important role. Reddish brown soil is considered to be the best followed by a tone of yellow. Dark or pungent smelling soil is not recommended. Any form of vegetation indicates that the soil is fertile and it shall be beneficial. To be sure, dig a pit measuring three cubic feet at the centre of the plot. After an hour fill it back with the excavated mud. If you observe a mound, the plot is auspicious, if it levels out, the plot is average and if there is a depression, the plot is infested with some negative energy, which must be negated before the construction begins. Otherwise living on such a plot could be unpleasant for all time to come.

Site selection

Many clients show the site layout to the architect and proceed with the building design. Traditionally, a consultant was involved in the choice of the site which may not be possible now. However, the following important aspects should be considered while choosing a site:

Shape of the plot

Which is the best shape for a plot? The earth has been assigned the symbolic shape of a square, hence, a square becomes the ideal shape for a plot. Somehow, in the current scenario it is not possible to purchase a square plot as they are not demarcated in that shape. A close second option is a rectangle, which too has all four sides at right angles: rather than a rhombus where the sides are either less

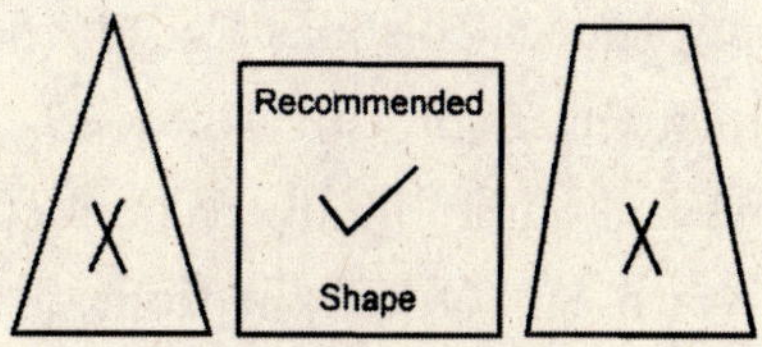

The best shape for a plot.

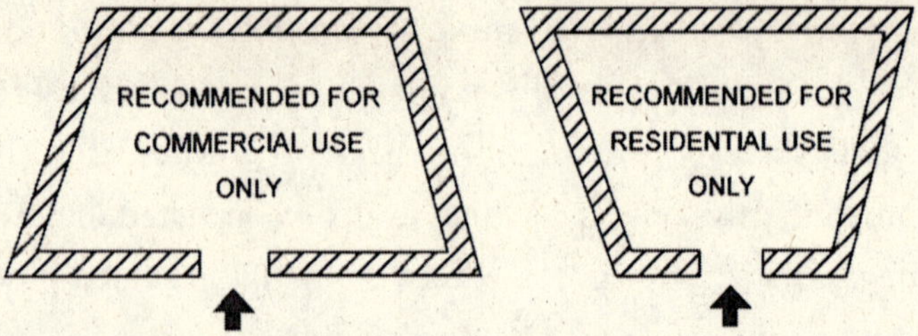

When the front of a house is narrower than the rear it is called *Gaumukh* and the reverse is called *Shermukh. Gaumukh* is excellent for residential purposes and *Shermukh* is recommended for commercial pusposes.

than or more than a right angle. A straight line represents unmanifest energy and the circle represents the manifest form. Circular plots/buildings are recommended for temples, hospitals or sports stadia, but not for residential or industrial purposes.

This could be the reason that in Delhi the circular Parliament building has too much energy, which cannot be handled by a single party.

Beware of a triangular plot

A triangle represents fire and is most suited for a restaurant. For all other activities, a triangular plot is not considered auspicious. This may lead the occupants to fight among themselves, or enter into litigation without any valid reason. Vaastu highly recommends an extension towards North-east. When the front of a house is narrower than the rear it is called *Gaumukh* and considered excellent whereas the reverse is called a *Shermukh,* excellent for commercial purposes. The direction of the extension is also very important.

In general a plot with an even number of sides is preferred over odd number of corners. However, if you can achieve any regular shape with a bifurcation of extended corners the plot becomes acceptable. (For more details read ***The Pocket Book of Vaastu*** also published by FULL CIRCLE.)

Odd-shaped plots are not considered auspicious for building in the Vaastu tradition. The actual plot needs to be defined either by means of a fence, a wall, or with pillars demarcating the boundary. The plot meant for construction should ideally be a geometric form such as a square or a rectangle and the remaining portion of the site may be used as a garden or a playground.

Claustrophobia could mean the pincer effect

The term 'pincer' is often used to mean squeezing something between two opposite points. This feeling of being squeezed can be experienced when you have a small plot between two larger ones. Not only do you get squeezed in, you also feel claustrophobic and your progress can be retarded in such a situation. It is advisable to negotiate your property with the plot owner to your South or West as they would benefit more by acquiring land towards North or East as they would extend in favourable directions and you would have the option of purchasing a better plot at an appropriate location that meets your requirement. The pincer effect of Vaastu is considered very inauspicious when the land or buildings on either side are larger or higher. It not only instills a feeling of inferiority but also blocks the free flow of positive *prana* and the sunlight from the East. In the eventuality of a structure existing between two tall buildings, Vaastu recommends the placing of mirrors on the roof to reflect back the negative energies.

The pincer effect.

Parallel roads can be very lucky

Any plot with parallel roads is lucky and with roads on two sides is considered good especially when they happen to be along North-east or South-west. When the roads are along North and West it is acceptable but South and East becomes tricky. When the roads are along three sides, it is considered to be lucky and prosperous. A plot with roads along all four sides fetches a premium as it brings in abundance and was earlier reserved for the king or the administrator. Most palaces had roads around them. When a house has an approach road towards North or East, North-west or South-east it is considered lucky. When the approach road is towards any other direction it may not be auspicious. Remember, there is a marked difference between an approach road and spearing road. The former brings in luck whereas the latter only causes unhappiness and discomfort.

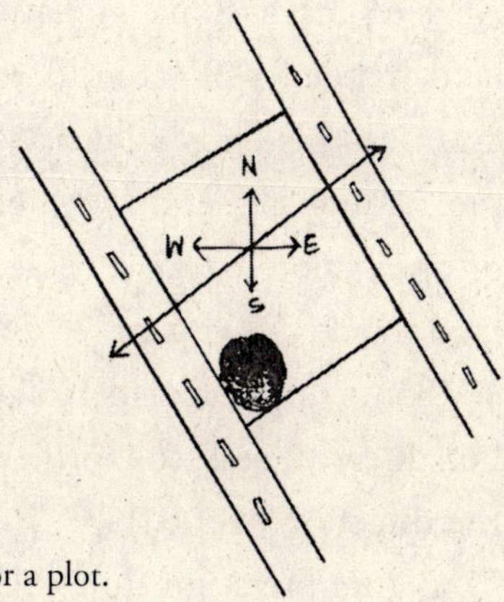

Considered good location for a plot.

Composition of earth, fertile soil ensures prosperity

The characteristics and composition of soil are very important for two reasons: one is the load-bearing capacity of the soil which defines the type of foundation to be constructed, the other is the ability of the land to sustain vegetation. The consultant would traditionally observe the site to ascertain whether the soil is fertile, holds water and sustains life forms such as plants, birds and animals. Any soil that is incapable of regeneration would be set aside as bad for human habitation. From an ecological point of view this analysis is extremely wise and can be added to the checklists.

Natural gradation

South-west to North-east brings abundance.

All sites have some gradation already existing in the land (refilled plots are different). The consultant has to examine this and build as sensitively as possible using the natural gradation. Water points, staircases, sewage disposal should take into account the gradation of the land, while designing.

Some slopes considered auspicious are South-west to North-east, South to North, and West to East. Whatever the direction of the slope, it must be utilised effectively. One interpretation for the importance of slopes in

Vaastu is that same direction of the slope is meant for each locality. This could well be a practical consideration where the water source and sewage is concerned so that the entire neighbourhood, village or city could have its waterways well-worked out.

Correct water source is a financial boon

The location of water on a site is one of the most important aspects of design. There are several ways in which water sources can be tapped. Ancient texts say water on the North or East is beneficial but when a water source is not possible or available in these two sides, any suitable location can be accepted. This is true for both individual buildings and for group housing. It is only logical that the natural slope of land, the water source and the collection of rain water would be linked. Water is also extracted through various methods, hence the location of good water in the proposed site or settlement is a cause for great jubilation. Its direction becomes secondary. A deep pit or a water tank in the North counterbalances a borewell in South-east or North-west.

Symmetrical dimensions bring harmony

A well-shaped object is pleasing to the eye, while anything out of proportion becomes an eyesore. Human beings are created with specific proportions and a similar scale of dimensions exist for houses. A 1:2 ratio for length and breadth is considered good with the height no more than the width. The above ratio also holds good for doors. Sleeping in a bedroom with four symmetrical walls can be blissful but six walls can make life a nightmare.

The Leaning Tower of Pisa and Qutab Minar are exceptions to the rule as they are not dwelling units. In multi-storeyed buildings the reference is to an individual flat, not the composite structure because the owners are different of different apartments and directions can also vary.

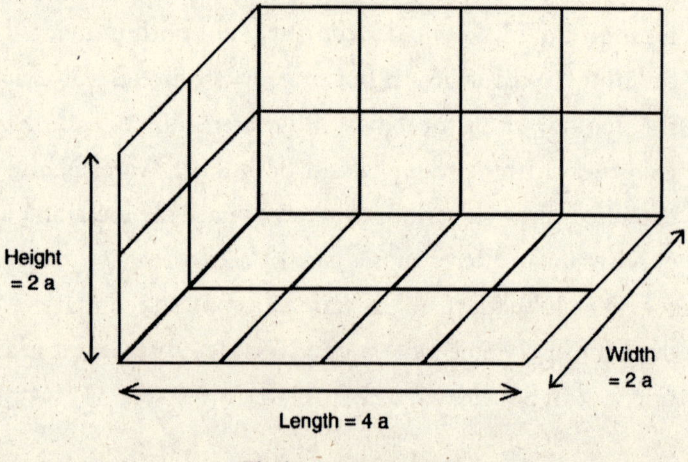

The best proportions.

Chapter Four

The Ideal Layout

Position

For long term happiness.

Ideally, construction should take place in the South-west quadrant of the plot leaving more space in the East as compared to the West, and more in the North as compared to the South. If this is not possible due to certain bye-laws of your state then you can ensure that East and North is at a lower level as compared to West and South, inside as well as outside the house/building. Also ensure that the centre of the plot and the house does not overlap.

Boundary wall

If your expenses are forever increasing check this wall.

The boundary wall along the South and West should be 12" higher than North and East i.e. if the wall is 6 ft. high towards East and North, then it should be 7 ft. towards South and West.

Main gate

It governs prosperity.

Depending upon which side your plot is facing, simply superimpose a *swastika* symbol on your plot. Wherever there is an opening in the *swastika,* you can place your main gate in the same area. It is best to place it near the central axis of the *swastika.*

Entrance door

It is also called Lakshmi Dwar.

The entrance door should not be directly in front of the main gate, as whatever comes in tends to flow out in this alignment.

Master bedroom

It governs relationships.

The ideal place for a master bedroom is in the South-west quadrant. It can also be along the South or the

West. South-east is generally not recommended as it is the quadrant of fire and a couple tends to be more argumentative when the master bedroom is built/placed in this corner. The North-west is recommended for newly married couples. Being the quadrant of air, it stimulates emotions as well as easy or early conception. For those planning a family the following tips can be useful:

- Before love making, the man should breathe through his right nostril (Sun *Pranayam)* for 15 minutes to enhance the chances of conceiving a male progeny. Similarly if the man breathes through his left nostril (Moon *Pranayam*) for 15 minutes the chances of begetting a female progeny is enhanced.
- Newly married couples should avoid having their bedroom towards the North-east corner of the house.

Children's bedroom

To discipline children their bedrooms should be in the appropriate direction.

It is preferable to have the children's bedroom along the North or East. North-west is best for girls and South-east for boys. The position of the bed should be in tandem with the East-West axis. The study table should be placed so that the child faces East and the tutor faces North. The recommended colour scheme for the room is light blue as it helps open up a child's mind to endless possibilities. Avoid the South-west corner for the children's bedroom.

For an excellent memory, study facing East

Study facing the East while placing your table in the North-east corner of the room with your bed towards the South or West. Sleeping with your head towards the East is excellent for memory recall.

A question often asked is, "Can we keep an image of Ganesha on our study table?" Ganesha symbolises prosperity which is measured by material wealth. When you study you enrich yourself with knowledge and become wiser not wealthier. Thus it would be better to place Ganesha on your work table and Saraswati on your study table as knowledge is the domain of this Goddess. You can enhance her vibrations by keeping a 100 gram rock crystal on a

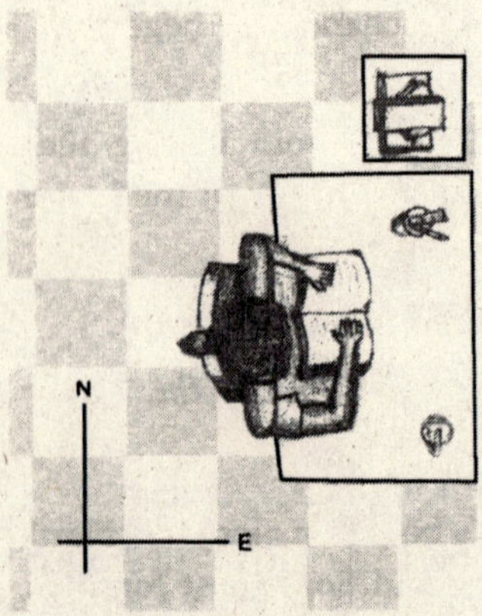

For better concentration, face the East while studying.

table which helps to focus, and which you may clean once a month with salt water.

Chant '*Om Hareeng Hasou Om Saraswatye Namah*' 108 times as soon as you wake up and before going to sleep. Burn sesame oil lamp towards the South wall and wipe the floor-with salt water for three days. Even simply chanting '*Om*', and feeling the vibrations in the forehead is excellent for memory.

Guest-room

It's lucky to have guests.

One does enjoy the company of guests as long as they shower blessings and good wishes on the family. However, the pleasure of their visit depends on the duration of their stay! The ideal location for the guest-room is the North-west, while the South-east is also acceptable. Avoid the South-west quadrant as such a house will always be full of guests. Light green is the colour for the guest-room as it induces compassion and consideration. Don't forget to keep an icon of Hanumanji in this room.

Elders room

Respect your elders and seek their blessings.

Although the South-west corner (quadrant) is recommended for the master bedroom, parents should exercise the first choice. In families where elders like uncles, aunts, or grandparents live together, the South-west quadrant is recommended for those not keeping good health. Their sleeping position remains the same as mentioned earlier. Lighting an oil lamp (mustard oil) in the South-east corner helps a great deal (for channelising positive health energies).

Place of worship

The ideal place of worship is in your heart.

The recommended location for this is the North-east quadrant of your house. The deity you worship can be facing East so that you face West while meditating. The ideal time for worship is between 4.00 a.m. - 6.00 a.m. and the ideal colour of the room is white. Those

God is always with you.

who do not believe in idol worship can also worship the rising sun.

Storeroom

Your progress can be choked by storing the wrong things.

More important than the direction of the storeroom is what you store in it. Objects which are used occasionally or seasonally are meant to be stored. Quite often we store things that we don't use for years and the room gets converted into a junk room and a junk room has no place inside a house! The storeroom can be along the southern or western side of the bedroom, kitchen or the house itself. Please do not keep pungent smelling articles inside your house. It is advisable to open your storeroom often enough to take stock of things. Anything which hasn't been used for three years or more is junk and must be removed or it will attract negative energies.

Kitchen

Health is governed by the placement of the kitchen.

Our body receives energy in the form of heat, light, the air we breathe, the water we drink and the food we eat. Obviously, the primary source of energy originates from the kitchen via food. It is advisable to build the kitchen along the South-east, East or South. The ideal zone for a kitchen lies in the South-east quadrant that houses the element of fire, having the symbolic shape of a triangle. Ideally, the sink should be towards the North-east, the cooking range or gas stove towards South-east and the refrigerator towards the South-west. This functional triangle has also been found to be most efficient. In most multi-storeyed apartments the kitchen does not have enough space for a triangular formation and the three objects are normally placed in a straight line. This is acceptable so long as the sink and gas stove are not in close proximity of one another as that could lead to friction within the family or profession. Increasing the gap between the sink and stove is recommended, otherwise you can place an image of Panchmukhi Hanuman*ji* between

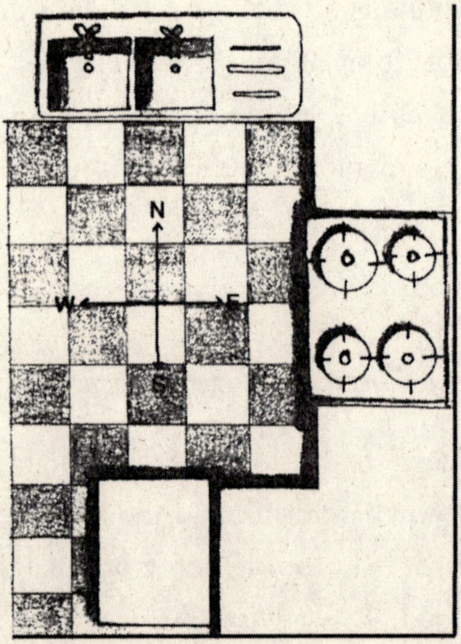

The primary source of energy originates from the kitchen via food. The best zone for a kitchen lies in the South-east quadrant. Ideally, the sink should be towards the North-east, the cooking range towards the South-east and the refrigerator towards the South-west. This functional triangle has been found to be most effective.

the two. The cook should ideally face the East, and the rations along the South stacked towards the West. The area must be well-lit, preventing any shadows from falling over the cooking vessels as it depletes the food of its *pranic* energy.

Finally the kitchen must be clean and hygienic. What really energises the food is the thought process of the person preparing the food. An angry cook always adds a little anger, a selfish cook would dress the dishes with selfishness, a dirty cook spikes the food with dirt. In other words, the character of the cook is always in the flavour, which induces similar traits in you. Hence, it's very important to prepare a meal with love, affection, care and hygiene as that is the stimulus we all require. Our grandmothers' specialities are always flavoured with blessings and goodness, which makes them very nourishing and tasty.

Toilet/Bathroom

They can spell disaster.

The traditional school of thought refers to the North-east as *Eshanaya* or the place of the gods. So a toilet, manhole or an open drain in the North-east can block the progress of dwellers and should be avoided. However, according to the modern school of thinking if there is a toilet in the

North-east you can take some remedial measures rather than demolishing it. For example, it may be sparingly used, you should always keep the seat cover down and place a small money plant along the North wall and a crystal towards the East wall. Ensure there is no water leakage.

Ideally one should take a bath with water at body temperature. Fill up a bucket of water and add a few drops of lime, this helps in cleaning the pores for easy exit of body toxins. While pouring water on your head with your left hand, gently rub your crown *chakra* (top of the head) with the finger-tips of your right hand. It's like a gentle massage and always chant the *Gayatri mantra.* Repeat this process 7 times. This helps in purifying the body and the mind. The ill effect of the toilet will be negated to a very large extent. The toilet door must always remain closed and a mirror fixed on it.

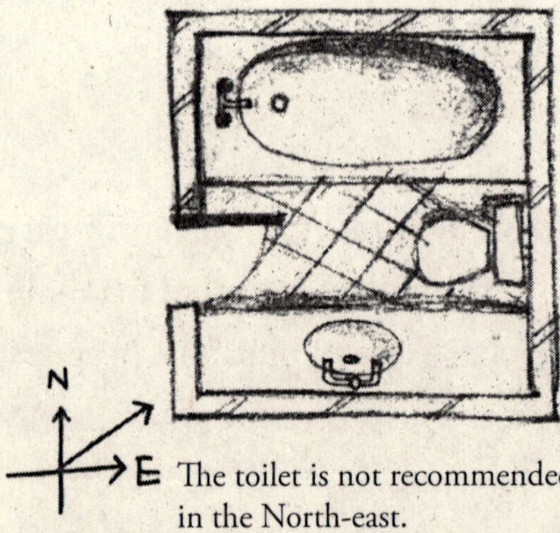

The toilet is not recommended in the North-east.

Don't wash your dirty linen in public. Not only should you refrain from offering others a sneak preview of your family affairs, you should avoid hanging the laundry in the front of your house. The sight of laundry is not pleasant and must be avoided as far as possible. It is best not to have a toilet where linen is washed right in front of or adjoining the main door. The toilet door must always be kept closed while washing.

To improve finances have a water feature in the North.

Sixty-six per cent of our planet's mass is water, the same percentage of water as our body has. Vaastu, therefore, emphasises on this element. Having a water source along the North-east quadrant can put your career on the right track. But when the underground water source storage is towards the South-east, not only does it create health problems, it also brews litigation and division in the family. When it is towards the South-west you will observe opportunities and health slipping out of your hands and when it is along the North-west your expenses will skyrocket and the children will be a cause for concern. Finally if it is placed towards the centre it mostly leads to bankruptcy.

Having a water source along the North-east quadrant can put your career on the right track.

Having the water source towards its prime direction is ideal but can be impractical. Therefore, install an alternate water feature along the North and reduce the ill effects of the existing source by encircling it with caustic soda or lime solution. Secondly, just like salt water (the sea) surrounds our planet, keep a bowl of salt water in the four corners of your house which notionally represents the above.

Chapter Five

The Magic of Vaastu

Vaastu cow

Once upon a time there was a farmer who had three sons. When he died he left behind 11 cows to be divided amongst his children. He had willed ½ the cattle to his eldest son, ¼ to the middle son and $^{1}/_{6}$ to his youngest son. The dilemma was how to divide a living cow. After quarrelling amongst themselves, the sons approached their uncle for help. He heard their story and contemplated for a while, then said, "I shall loan you my Vaastu cow which you

The mystic cow.

must return after sorting out the problem." The sons agreed and all four of them returned to the village with the Vaastu cow. The uncle asked how many cows there were including the cow he had loaned them. Twelve, they answered. He said the eldest son takes ½ that is 6, the middle son takes ¼ that is 3, and the youngest takes $^1/_6$ that is 2. And that adds up to 6+3+2 = 11. Happily the uncle returned to his house along with his Vaastu cow.

Note: Vaastu cow is just an expression.

Are all the directions favourable for everyone?

Directions and their energies have a stimulating effect. We cannot see them, yet they help to sort out problems and create harmony. Vaastu is all about directional orientations which add a new dimension to life.

Maximise good luck for travel — Choose the direction, then the day.

Vaastu has assigned directions to respective planets and each represents one day of the week. Sunday morning favours the East, Friday favours the South-east, Saturday the West and Sunday evening favours the South-west. Monday — North-west, Tuesday – South, Wednesday — North and Thursday — North-east. It is good to start the day along its favourable direction but this does not mean you travel in a different direction every day! Obviously this is impractical as your place of work is fixed with respect to your house and so is the direction. Therefore, the best way to appease the planet of the day is simply to look towards its direction and begin your journey. Conflict and contradiction are a part of life but there might be days when you experience them more. If you analyse which days these are, finding a solution becomes easier.

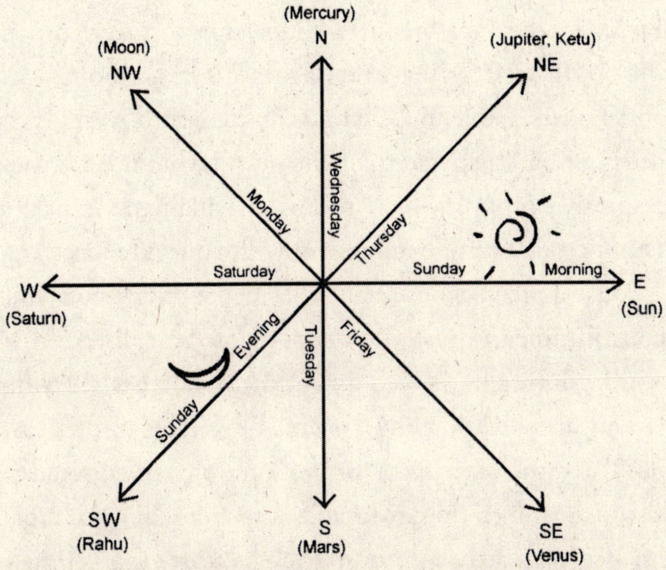

Vaastu has assigned directions to respective planets and each planet dominates one day of the week.

A lot of research is carried out to establish the link between the planets and their corresponding directions. Although a planetary phase is always in transition, the location of a planet with respect to directions is now taken as constant. For instance, we have Jupiter and Ketu in the North-east, the Sun in the East, Venus in the South-east, Mars in the South, Rahu in the South-west, Saturn in the West, Moon in the North-west and Mercury in the North. These are fixed and do not change as per Vaastu. When the twelve signs of zodiac, are divided amongst the four directions of Vaastu, it gives three signs per quadrant. These have been classified as Cancer, Scorpio, Pisces in the North-east, Gemini, Virgo, Capricorn in the South-west, Aries, Leo, Sagittarius in the South-east and Taurus, Libra and Aquarius in the North-west. These directions are also said to be the most favourable for their respective groups which means the main door or the entrance gate can be in tandem with your direction.

Just as you choose your diet depending upon your constitution so must you choose your best direction. A 1500 calorie diet is recommended by doctors but what if you are an athlete? It would be totally insufficient. Similarly the activity or profession you are engaged in also determines the favourable directions. For example, finance is North, administration is East, marketing is North-west, production is South-west or South-east, creativity or R&D is South-east, authority is South-west, entertainment and nightclubs is West, education is East and so on. Therefore, it would not be wise to reject a South or West-facing property and put an unrealistic premium on North/East facing one because if South and West are bad then why is the master bedroom or CEO's office recommended here?

Lunar and solar currents

For abundance and longevity control.

Ida and *Pingala* are the lunar and solar currents. Our left nostril represents *Ida* and the right *Pingala.* These currents are drawn into our lungs when we breathe for onward distribution to the various organs and systems. Similarly, a house draws these currents from nature, the right side (East) of the house represents solar (masculine) and the left side (West) represents the lunar (feminine). If there is a Vaastu *dosha* (block) on the left side, it will

Ida and *Pingala* of your house.

affect the female members whereas a *dosha* on the right side is likely to affect the male members. The impact of these *doshas* can be on health, profession, relationships, prosperity; or any other area depending upon its location. You can circumvent the same with reorientation of the layout to improve the energy flow and make the house more vibrant.

Chapter Six

Energy Flows

Treat your house like your body

Vaastu recommends you treat your house like your body. Gautama Buddha said to treat your body like a house. He said the soul keeps changing its house while searching for the house builder. Once it finds the house builder (ego) further houses are built. Does it imply there is life after life or that we keep changing our body in this life? Medical science will support the theory that our body changes its cellular structure every seven years which means our physical body undergoes a complete transformation at least 10 times in a life span of 70 years. While we are constantly in the process of change we forget to look at the constant because we are driven by our *vaasnas* (desires), that are supported by our ego. We usually forget *vaastava* (universal reality).

People invest so much time and money on their physical appearance everyday with the aim of looking good. But do they spend even half of that time on beautifying their home? It is important to have beautiful interiors as well as exteriors. Some ways to ensure this is to make certain that the walls and furniture are smooth and well polished. Ceilings and walls with paint peeling off or chipped plaster attract bad luck and ill health into your house. Water seepage is just as bad, if not worse. The ancient Indian tradition of whitewashing the house before every Diwali was not just a fad, it was a very meaningful exercise. Paints and wall finishes last upto five years now but this should not prevent us from following ancient tradition. If not the whole house, at least the kitchen and toilets should be whitewashed or painted every year. The texture of the walls should be as smooth as your skin for good luck.

Well-lit interiors

Black is a good absorber and a good radiator of heat. It absorbs a lot of light and depletes us of our energies. Black holes are areas on earth (The Bermuda Triangle) and in the universe which suck in anything within their range. We get the same effect in excessively dark areas in our homes. In such a situation our energies are depleted, resulting in depression and sickness. The house must always be properly lit, especially the entrance and the passages. Children are always afraid of darkness, and fear or nervousness are experienced when a home or office is poorly lit. Similarly, dark clothes are worn in winter whereas in summers they look heavy. This reminds me of a showroom done up by a designer in black and copper. Though these colours are acceptable in the West due to their climatic conditions, they generally do not attract customers in tropical countries. Imagine walking into a showroom with a black ceiling. Fear or unease will accompany you, no matter what you are purchasing. Ceilings should always be white and well lit so that your house or shop does not appear to be a black hole.

Light affects your mood.

Choose favourable colours — they add value to life

Each direction has a favourable colour, which may be added to enhance a particular energy. For example, the most compatible colour for the East is golden yellow, white or lemon green. For the West it's all half tones such as grey or electric blue. Even metallic colours such as gold, silver and copper are found to be very suitable. For the North the best is green, blue or turquoise while for the South it is red, yellow, orange, pink or magenta. When I mention suitable colours it does not mean one must have rooms of different colours in each direction or walls of different colours in a room, it simply indicates the need for a prominent article of that colour in its favourable direction. The ideal colour for walls is white or any pastel shade. Avoid dark walls and ceilings because happiness remains clouded.

False ceiling and basement can lead to depression

Does Vaastu recommend false ceilings? There is no reference to false ceilings in the ancient texts as it is a modern concept. In the good old days, *havelis* and palaces had high ceilings to prevent heat from getting blocked inside the rooms. This is also supported scientifically by the fact that warm air rises up, so a room with a high ceiling would create a layer in which the upper part would be warm and the lower always remain cool. The evolution of construction saw a decline in the concept of having a high ceiling to achieve more covered area at low cost. A low ceiling can make the room quite uncomfortable specially during the monsoon as cooling machines become ineffective. This gave rise to the necessity of a false ceiling. On the top floor it keeps the heat out and also gives the room an aesthetic look. Actually any room with exposed beams should have a false ceiling to ward off the pressure or negative effect of the beam. If there is a beam running across a bedroom then a false ceiling is a must. Avoid a basement under a room with a false ceiling as there should not be a false ceiling and false flooring in the same room.

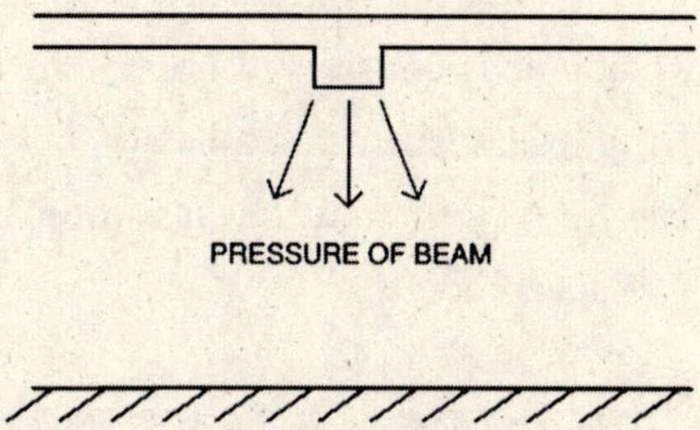

If you have a beam running across your bedroom then a false ceiling is a must. But do avoid a basement under a room with a false ceiling as you should not have a false ceiling and false flooring in the same room.

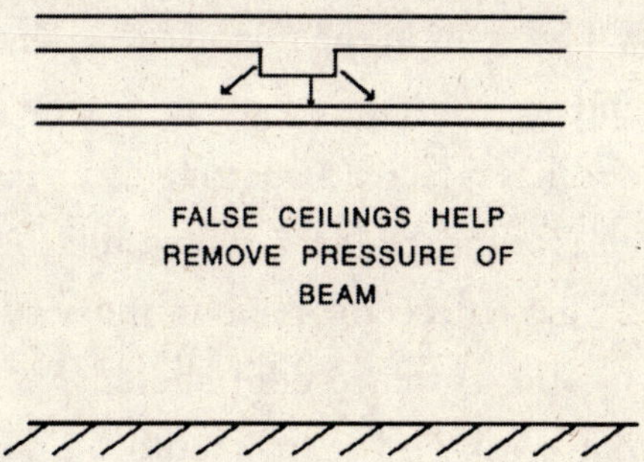

Should a building have a basement or not? From a builder's point of view there should be no restriction. Traditionally a basement was used as a cellar. A basement should be brightly lit with cross ventilation and proper treatment against water seepage. It should have large windows to allow maximum light and fresh air to make it functional. A dingy basement may be used for storage only. A basement towards the North-east is auspicious as it brings good luck. If it is towards the South-east it leads to litigation and division, if towards the North-west it increases expenses and if towards the South-west it affects business, health and relationships. A full basement is considered good. The recent excavation of King Akbar's Summer Palace below the courtyard in Fatehpur Sikri stands as testimony that a full basement was acceptable.

Your house has a face too!

Keep it smiling. The face is the index of your mind. Whatever is in the mind is generally reflected on the face and we constantly fight to hide it. Likewise your house also has a face. In apartments or flats it's the front door and for independent houses, it is the entrance gate which always reflects the mind of the occupants.

The entrance door should not have cracks, should not creak and there should be no trash can inside or outside the entrance door. Very often people keep their dustbins right outside the door either for the convenience of the sweepers or they find that to be the most

convenient spot. Find an alternate place and always cover the dustbin. If there is a parapet or a porch above the door it should not be used to store junk. That is like dandruff and must be removed.

Generate positive vibrations to attract happiness

Whatever we see, hear, touch, taste and smell becomes part of our existence, hence, it should be pleasant. It is, therefore, recommended not to hang paintings depicting war, crime, agony, distress or discomfort of any sort. Also avoid storing objects or articles that give you bad vibrations. Stop using broken or chipped crockery, especially teacups and glasses.

Beauty lies in the eyes of the beholder. Yet certain objects are not beautiful no matter who sees them. Dead or withering plants should never be kept in front of the house or in the balcony as they accumulate negative *prana* and should be disposed off. When you magnify the above statement it is equivalent to keeping a corpse at home. The law does not permit that. Similarly, the law of Vaastu does not permit the keeping of perished plants or flowers. At times people have lifeless trees in their gardens, they are emotionally so attached to them that removing them is not acceptable. In such a situation growing creepers to simulate life on the tree is recommended. And until the creeper embraces the entire tree, a bamboo wind chime or flute can be hung to generate positive vibrations.

Think half glass full.

Harness natural elements

Our planet has enough natural resources to fulfill every man's need but not enough to fulfill one man's greed! This greed can eventually lead to the depletion of natural resources as happened recently with the indiscriminate felling of trees all over the world culminating in El Nino's devastating effect. The wise realised not to play with nature and trees were planted throughout the world to overcome the crisis. With the evolution of technology we find numerous man-made products using organic raw materials being substituted by synthetic products, for instance engine oil, fabrics, dyes, pigments and now a common sight in every home — artificial plants. Vaastu

The law of Vaastu does not permit the keeping of dead plants. At times people are attached to lifeless trees in their gardens. In such a situation growing creepers to simulate life on the tree is recommended.

strongly opposes the use of synthetic plants specially indoors as they have a negative aura which depletes yours. They do not release oxygen that generates *pranic* energy inside the house. Therefore, if you are fond of artificial flowers make sure they are made of silk but never of plastic. Such plants should be kept outside the house or between a cluster of natural plants.

Metal beds can make you restless

Like the evolution of mankind we find building materials have also evolved from mortar and stone bricks to prefabricated slabs, engineering plastics and reinforced metals. Not only the materials but even the interiors of our homes have taken a quantum leap. Take for instance the bed which was once a stone block covered with straw or animal skin, then a *charpai* having a wooden frame with a mesh of jute or coir woven on it, to box beds and now we have wrought iron beds which look very elegant but dispel the magnetic currents in the body. Vaastu does not suggest you dispense with your metal bed, but recommends that you keep a wooden plank between the metal grid and the mattress. Moreover, these metal beds are best kept in a West-facing bedroom, and should be avoided in the East and South.

4 is the lucky number for stability

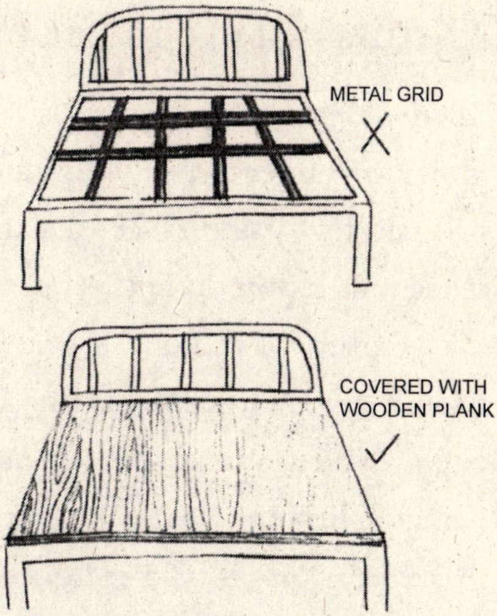

Vaastu recommends placing a wooden plank between the metal grid and mattress on your metal bed. These beds are best kept in a West-facing bedroom.

Stability is a virtue of the earth and has a symbolic representation in the shape of a square. What could be better than a four-legged chair for people in authority. Beware of a swivel or reclining chair that can have a similar effect on your career. Your dining table must be on four legs, never three, and your bed also called a *charpai,* should have *char* (four) *pai* (legs). Due to paucity of space people can use a box bed but use it to store only linen or warm clothes. If you keep toys, crockery or cutlery don't blame your stars for your back problems. A box bed that cannot be cleaned underneath collects negative energies and causes poor health. It is recommended you raise the bed by keeping bricks in the four corners or fix 4-inch wooden pegs under it. Please ensure the floor is wiped everyday for good health to return.

Mirrors can expand or repel fortunes

Mirror, mirror on the wall, who is the prettiest of them all? How do you feel when you stand in front of a mirror? It is said that you first see your inner-self and then your reflection. If you do not feel good in front of a mirror, ask yourself why? Look at the mirror and make sure it's not chipped or broken and doesn't have any sharp edges. Never look at yourself in a cracked mirror as it would split your image into bits. Do not see yourself in a mirror that is oxidized or has a spotty surface (this includes coloured glass). Also make sure that the mirror is so placed that your face does not get cut off in the mirror. You should be able to see at least 6 inches above your head as it ensures growth. Placement of the mirror is also important. In the toilet it should be above the wash-basin (which is preferred along the North wall) while decorative mirrors can be hung anywhere.

Make sure your mirror is not chipped, broken or has any sharp edges. Never look at yourself in a cracked mirror.

Activate the North-west zone to overcome dullness

Gati (movement) is the essence of life. When anything becomes static (stagnant) it creates discomfort, whether it is at work or in the family. A static environment is not conducive to growth. It must become dynamic i.e. converting static energy to kinetic by adding bright colours or removing dull/dark shades, putting in plants or placing mirrors. In the good old days bronze bells were used, today we can also use functional music. For instance, the sound of wind chimes is excellent. The North-west is the zone of *gati.* Supplement all your efforts by activating the North-west zone of your house

RAKESH CHAWLA

or factory by cleaning and clearing the junk. Remember, whenever movement stops, it creates restlessness. So your efforts must be directed towards activating the North-west quadrant.

Avoid straight lines to curtail expenses

There are no short cuts to success. It is always a long and tedious road with ups and downs, which help us to digest the sweet taste of success. This is akin to our digestive system as the intestinal tract is zigzag and not a straight passage. Likewise, in our house the passage connecting the main entrance to the rear door should not be in a straight line as whatever comes in shall find its way out, without being digested. Your expenses shall always be the same, if not more than your income, with only a remote possibility of any savings.

For the same reason, avoid having three doors in a straight line. The passages in the house should be well defined and clear. Do not have too many objects (obstacles) along the passage as they hamper the flow of energy. When a door at the end of a corridor is opening into a bedroom/office cabin, it is not considered good. Place a mirror at eye level.

In addition to a straight passage if you have a staircase right at the entrance it could be troublesome, because Vaastu translates ego as a rise in energy level, which is physically represented by a staircase. The sight of a linear staircase at the entrance of any building or house reinforces the ego of the occupants, hence, it is recommended to tone down the effect by camouflaging the same with plants and fixing a mirror next to it. Please remember positive ego (self esteem) is essential for our survival but negative (fake) ego must go.

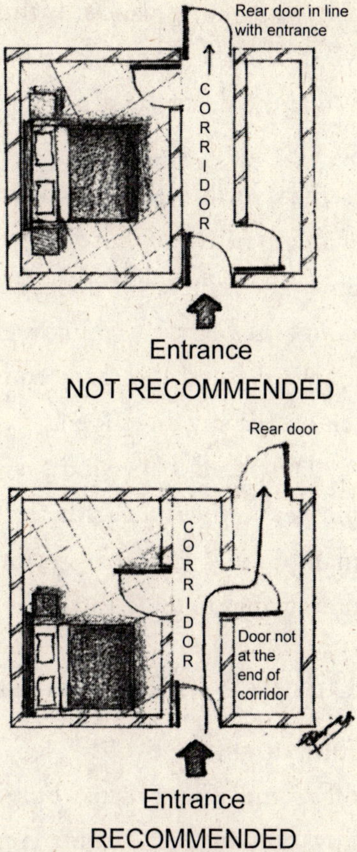

Avoid doors in a straight line.

Doors and windows are the eyes and ears

What is the ideal number of doors and windows? The traditional school of Vaastu puts a premium on an even number of doors and the same number of windows. In modern buildings windows do not have a single panel, but two or three panels. Is this to be considered a single window or should one panel be equivalent to one window? While the debate is still on, it is recommended we have an open and larger surface area of doors and windows facing North-east as compared to the South-west to enable positive *pranic* energy to permeate the dwelling unit. The number of doors and windows should reduce as you rise higher in a building or their size should reduce marginally and the main door should be located in the left half of any direction as seen from inside the house.

French or bay windows do not come under this purview as they add aesthetic value. A single panel square main door is very inauspicious whereas a double panel door brings in good fortune.

Diffused lighting is harmonious

All that glitters is not gold. As you enter a shop or an office and find a naked bulb glaring into your eyes — how do you feel? A study conducted by a large lighting company found that glare, not only causes irritability, it also reduces efficiency whereas on roads it can cause accidents. Glare creates light pollution and no one likes pollution of any sort.

While good light is important it should never cause a glare. Indirect lighting diffused from the ceiling has a very soothing effect because it resembles daylight. If

Avoid glare.

you have any naked bulbs, make sure they are shaded, especially in your bedroom. The entrance to your house or shop should be bright, not glaring, and a bright image of Ganesha or Gajlaxmi on the main door is considered very auspicious.

Coolers and air-conditioners can block your finances

With the onset of summer, coolers and air-conditioners are a boon, and sales are brisk. But mechanics install them in any conceivable window. Though these machines have no reference in the ancient scriptures as they were invented only a few decades ago, Vaastu recommends to place them along the North-west and South-east corresponding to their displacement of air and heat respectively. Coolers must be removed after the season because when not in use they prevent the natural light from penetrating inside. This can retard your progress by creating static current. Make sure coolers do not have stagnant water or your finances can get stagnant. Hence, it is best to cover the cooler with a polythene sheet and keep it in the storeroom or on the roof. Air-conditioners on the other hand do not take much space nor block the light from coming in so they need not be removed during winter.

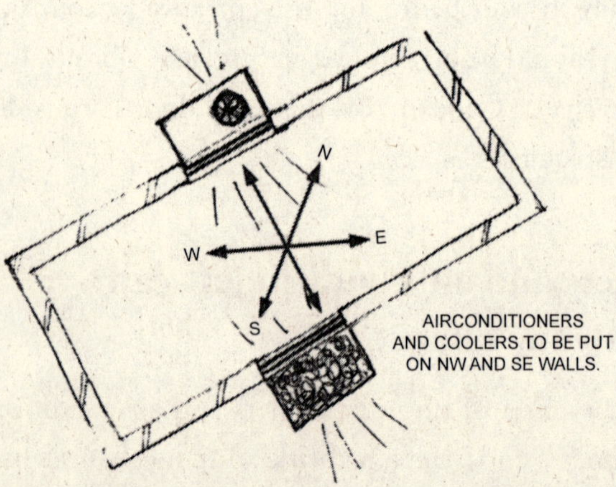

Vaastu recommends that coolers be put away after the summer season as they prevent natural light from penetrating inside a room.

Your *tajori* should face North!

The slogan "small is beautiful" is very popular as we can see everything shrinking in size, be it houses, cars, computers, even money (credit cards). The concept of credit cards is new and finds no reference in the ancient text that speaks of a treasury or a safe to keep coins and jewellery along the South wall opening towards North. Vaastu recommends keeping your valuables such as credit cards, cash and jewellery in a cupboard that faces North, the direction of Lord Kuber and of wealth. Do not keep your expensive perfumes on the same shelf because perfume evaporates and so can your wealth. You should not keep documents pertaining to your property or FDRs, bonds, share certificates because they are neither cash nor jewellery. All these should be kept separately, maybe in your office. Vaastu says if your cash box faces South or West your expenses shall always be more than the income. Change its direction right away.

Cupboard storing valuables should face North.

How to increase your savings through Vaastu? There are two ways to save. Either you reduce your expenses or increase your income. For a working executive, increasing income can largely be at the hands of dishonesty, which Vaastu does not recommend. To increase your savings Vaastu suggests checking wasteful expenditure. Where you spend is best known to you and your spouse. To find out whether you are incurring wasteful expenditure or not, check the leaking taps in your bathrooms, kitchen, balconies or garden. If you find any, it definitely indicates you have been wasteful. Sealing off the leakage will help a great deal. Now for those in business, cutting costs is the best option but it does get difficult, hence, they also must look for leaking taps. To increase the income, activating a water feature, like an aquarium, towards the North can work wonders. Also make sure the cash box and cupboard in which the valuables are kept is facing North or East.

Anyone who wants to improve his financial wealth, should place an image of Ganesha or Gajlaxmi on the main door, adding a small water feature towards the North of the house, a *tulsi* towards the East, *neem* towards the West and chant *Om Kareeng Hareeng Shreeng Laleeng Hasou Jagthprasutye Namah* 108 times a day. Notice the changes in 41 days.

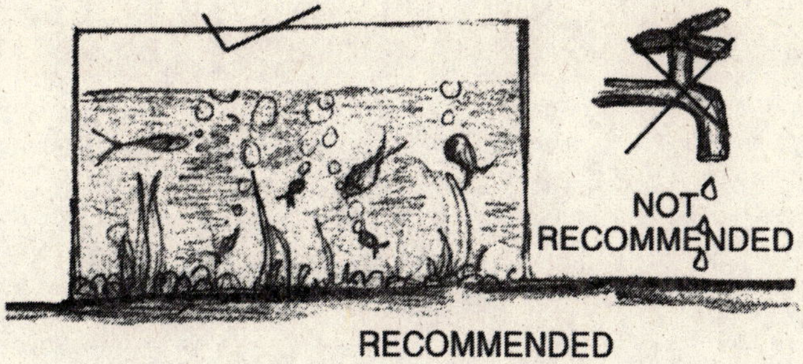

Water represents money.

To enhance your supply of money, you can also place money plants on either side of your front door plus install a water feature towards the North-east and do wash your feet before retiring to bed at night.

Chapter Seven

Career

Work smart

On sound values and self-confidence lies the foundation of your career. Make sure it is strong. It pays more than working hard. Many a time one wonders how directional orientations can have such an impact on our existence. After all there is no substitute for hard work. Ancient wisdom says there is nothing like smart work. We all have great potential and are blessed with many gifts, the only thing holding us back is self doubt. This doubt or lack of confidence is the key to many locks. We must realise our potential and use our talents to pursue the right career. When our career is in conformity with our potential, we work smart. If not, we always have to work

One must realise his/her potential and what one is gifted with to pursue the right career.

hard and remain dissatisfied with the results. These days, it's not only grades which help you to get a job, it is self-confidence. To enhance it, sit in tandem with the axis that is along South facing the North or along the West facing the East. Always wear colours that make you feel vibrant, and most important of all look at yourself in a full length mirror with the lights focused on you. I have found this in the dressing rooms of most successful people.

Girls can be smarter than boys

With the opening up of our economy many MNCs have opened shop and also created new job opportunities.

The last decade has witnessed an increase in the number of working women, specially in North India. Girls from middle class families are found to be most ambitious and lead the field in many careers such as fashion, beauty and the media. *What is the role of Vaastu in this phenomenon*? The umbrella of creativity, which is directionally inclined towards South-east, North-west, has the ruling planet Venus as lord of the quadrant. Whenever women excel in any field their South-east is found to be in perfect harmony and complemented by the North-west quadrant of air with the moon as the lord. Both these planets, Venus and moon, are feminine in nature whereas fire and air have a positive

Girls are smarter.

charge that can be extremely favourable to women. Those of you who want to excel should have your bedroom towards the North-west and study or office towards the South-east. Coming into the limelight can just be a thought away.

Make sure your boat sails

Life without a goal is like a boat without a rudder. The boat in which we sail through life is our house and the rudder is the rear portion. Very often we neglect the rear part thinking it has no value as it is not seen by visitors and sparingly visited by the occupants. The rudder of the house often becomes a junkyard. This also holds good for factories and large offices.

Please ensure that this does not happen specially if your house faces South or West. Instead of neglecting this portion develop a kitchen garden or a beautifully landscaped nursery. If you follow this you shall experience

Clear the clutter for a smoother flow.

new openings in life as a lot of blocks will get removed. To enhance your career prospects, place a small water feature towards the North or Last and please reaffirm your goals as your boat is now ready to sail. Visualising your goals before you sleep helps in achieving them.

Chapter Eight

Office

CEO's cabin

Are Vaastu principles the same for homes and offices? While the basic parameters remain the same, the difference in activities needs a little attention. For instance, in a house, the master bedroom is recommended towards the South-west. Similarly a CEO's cabin is also suggested in the same zone. The cabin should be a regular shape of a square or rectangle, and rooms with corners cut off or having an odd number of walls must be avoided. While it is recommended to sleep with your head towards the South, it is best to face the East at the work tables, as the rising sun being the ruler of the planets enlightens us the most. It may inspire you to radiate similar energies in your activities. To face the North is considered auspicious for those in finance, accounts, stocks and shares or any financial services.

The entrance must be bright for Laxmi and Ganesha to be happy

The entrance is best defined as a transition from one energy level to another. Just as the entrance to your house should be bright and vibrant, the same holds good for your office where the reception area plays an important role. If the entrance door opens to a dead wall a few feet away and the area is dark or gloomy it may mean that all your efforts are not reaping the desired results. Placing a mirror on such a wall not only adds a feeling of space, any visitor harbouring negative energies will drop them when he catches his reflection in the mirror and these negative energies can be picked up by large crystal bowls filled with salt water or rose petals. Flowers and natural plants are found to be equally effective. A statue or image of Ganesha, the lord of prosperity, on the reception table is very auspicious and when accompanied by Goddess Laxmi, the doors of fortune open.

Create the right ambience for success

In today's corporate culture everyone is striving for success and the price one pays is devoting more time to the office than to the family. The guilt one carries is reflected in areas of life like poor interpersonal relationships, lack of teamwork and low motivation. Thus it is of prime importance to create the right ambience at your place of work. Ambience is not only aesthetics, but also the rhythm which creates a resonance between the objectives of the company and the mindset of the employees. Vaastu recommends correct placement and directional alignment, regular shapes, pleasing colour combinations etc. If you sit with your back towards the entrance to your cubicle rest assured your colleagues are conspiring against you and may literally stab you in the back! If your glass table top is broken you are fighting against all odds. Replace it.

Focus on your people for more profit

In marketing, there is a saying "Customer is King" and because of stiff competition everyone focuses on customer service. Corporate houses adopting Kaizen's approach use the '5 M's' to identify a problem. These are : Man, Machine, Material, Method and Measurement. It is interesting to note that other than man, the remaining four may be similar to what the competitors use. To be ahead of competition, your focus should be on human beings who have a mind of their own and respond to their surroundings. To increase the efficiency of human beings you have to offer a conducive work environment which Vaastu recommends. In Europe and America, a lot of companies have incorporated an environmental aspect as part of HR as they feel human beings are the strongest assets of a company. Their workplace must have an ambience incorporating the best direction, colours, forms and dimensions. Needless to say the results are amazing.

Solutions for your problems are in realigning directions

The core issues in any business are operational, financial, legal, marketing and production, and their corresponding directions are South-west, North-east, South-east, North-west and Cen tre/West with the corresponding elemental energies being earth, water, fire, air and space. Vaastu suggests we first identify the problem then focus along its direction to remove the block. This can appear as a corner being cut off or unproportionately ex tended. It could be un even floor

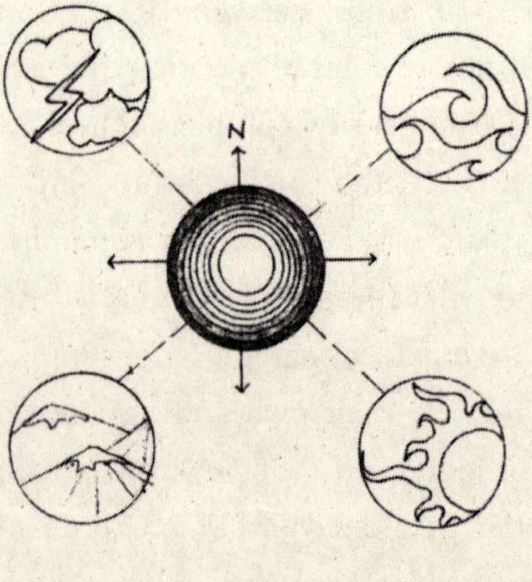

Identify the activity to its corresponding direction.

levels or too many columns in the production hall or ad ministration building and finally if all the machine operators are facing South or West, the breakdown and rejection rate could be fairly high. Before incorporating any changes please get rid of all rusted and unusable parts, realign your work direction and ensure the lighting levels conform to the norms of the industry. Different floor levels inside a production hall can cre ate havoc.

Embrace creative visualisation for stress management

Of late many motivational seminars and personal development workshops have become the buzzword in the corporate world. The pressure of competition is taking its toll on its employees so intensely that a number of executives are reeling under stress or cardiac disorders. The power of creative visualisation has been found to be extremely effective and can be practiced with regulated breathing. Vaastu says, breathing is the only link between your physical and mental being, so when you regulate your breathing, your mind automatically comes under your control. In any organisation where employees are prone to stress please ensure they do not sit facing one another or very close to exit doors. They should never sit under a beam or near a column and finally, if the edge of a table or a wall points towards them, the employees would soon be pointing their fingers at the management.

Recognise different vibrations

You could also form a habit of walking around in your office or factory. It is very important to know exactly what is happening in every nook and corner of your business premises. Ensure junk is not collected, seepage, leaking taps and broken window panes are repaired immediately. According to Vaastu the above can cost you physical, mental and emotional unrest. By regularly walking around you start recognising the negative vibrations and learn to correct the same. This exposure to different vibrations is as important as formal education which adds to your experience. Sitting and working at the same place for long hours can be very boring or stressful, thus walking around can help in many ways.

A turtle can do wonders

Slow and steady wins the race.

In Vaastu parlance God is described as Generator (Brahma), Operator (Vishnu), and Destroyer (Shiva). According to Hindu mythology, Vishnu will have ten incarnations, the last known was Krishna and the tenth will be Kalki. In one of his forms he appeared as a turtle. The CEO or departmental head of any organisation can be functionally equated to Vishnu and for his energies to transcend, it is recommended to keep a crystal or ceramic turtle towards the right. His table/cabin should not be at the end of a passage or corridor, particularly with the door opening right in front. The traits of Brahma are bestowed on the production head with Shiva looking upon HRD as the destroyer of fear and ignorance amongst employees. Your backbone (spine) is the pillar of strength, so ensure it is firmly rested against a high back chair with a wall behind. Please avoid a window at the back.

All divisional heads are advised not to have their cabins at the end of a long corridor and they must sit on high back chairs having a wall behind supporting the image of their supreme being or hang a picture of a mountain but no water.

Ganesha makes your stocks soar

When share prices zoom investors make money (notionally) and feel it's their intelligence and wise decision that works

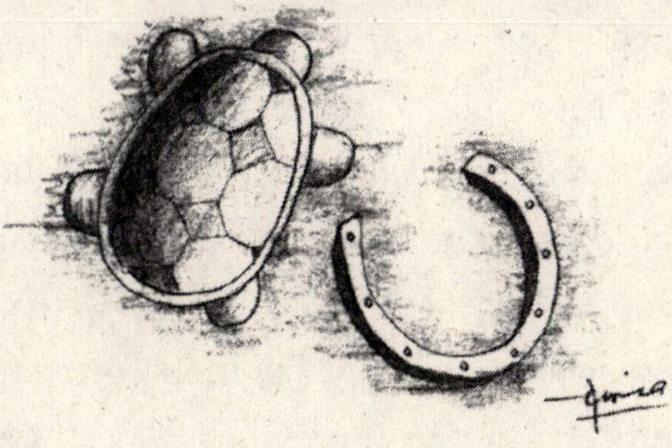

Lucky Charms: A horse-shoe or ceramic turtle can help the departmental head of an organisation to function more efficiently.

whereas when the market crashes, investors and brokers want to ascertain whether their offices have the right vibrations! Are they facing the right direction? Is the computer placed correctly? Investment in stocks is risky and the thumb rule is — the higher the risk, the more the gain or vice versa. Vaastu does not propagate speculation but recommends we work along favourable directions like North or East. Having the monitor towards these directions shall help you take sensible decisions which most likely will be profitable. However, if the monitor faces West or South, the temptation to hold on and the urge to make more money transcends as these are directions for entertainment, not profit making. Keeping an image of Ganesha and Gajlaxmi is strongly recommended for those in the stocks and shares business.

Bronze bells and metal wind chimes can improve sales!

Can Vaastu help to improve sales? Yes! Irrespective of what you sell, the zone associated with sales and marketing is North west, which houses the element of air. Movement is the virtue of air and whenever it stops you feel uncomfortable. The same holds good for the products you sell where lack of movement causes worry and anxiety. The easiest way to activate this element is by placing a metallic fan in its zone and to hasten up the process hang six bronze bells or a six cylinder metal wind chime. The vibration of this sound attracts customers. You can also enhance the vibration of this area by installing an image of Hanuman*ji* often referred to as V*ayuputra.* In any office the North-west corner can be assigned to the marketing head. In a shop, slow moving stocks may be kept in this corner. A Sri Yantra in this corner can also be a boon.

Chapter Nine

Health

Get rid of junk from your house and mind

Summer brings with it not just a variety of mangoes but also prickly heat and irritability. Excess of toxins in our body create discomfort, even diseases, but they can, fortunately, be flushed out by having 10-12 glasses of water everyday. But what about the toxins that we create, in the form of junk which accumulates in our houses. It is good to have a storeroom along the South or West where one can put away things that are used occasionally. Anything that has not been used in the last five years and that is not likely to be used in the next five years is 'junk' and Vaastu does not recommend a junk room in any house/factory/ shop. Also check all that you have collected in your cupboards, drawers and most importantly, in your handbags and wallets. If you don't clear the physical toxins on a regular basis, irritability is bound to trouble you through the year and no amount of lotions will be of any help. If you cannot clear the physical junk then clearing your negative feelings and emotions is next to impossible.

Sleep with your head towards the South for blissful sleep

We're all familiar with the saying: "An apple a day keeps the doctor away." Homes which are perpetually sickness ridden need special attention. I believe physical sickness first sets in the mind and then manifests itself in the body. You need a healthy mind in order to have a healthy body. Restful sleep is very important to ensure a healthy mind. How many hours a day do you sleep? Six to eight hours is recommended. If you find it difficult to sleep, try changing the position of your head. Ideally, aduits should sleep with their heads towards the South. North is generally not recommended though some people sleep like babies with their heads towards the North. The theory of magnetism supports the view that opposite poles attract and similar poles repel. The head of the human body is considered the north. That's why it is advisable to sleep with the head towards the South. When we sleep with our head towards the North the repulsion in magnetic currents takes place which can cause blood related disorders like BP, cholesterol or insomnia. These can easily be controlled by regulating your diet, sleeping habits and sleeping direction.

Children are advised to sleep with their heads towards the East. West is a standby although some consider it inauspicious to sleep with their feet towards the rising sun specially if there is a window on the eastern wall. Sleeping in a room with too many metal cupboards should be avoided and sleeping under the beam is out of the question.

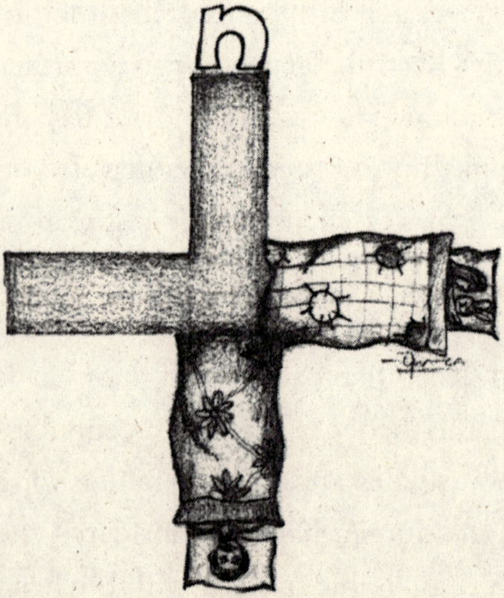

Sleep Right: Ideally, adults should sleep with their heads towards the South. Blood related disorders like BP, cholesterol and insomnia can be controlled by regulating diet, changing your sleeping habits and the direction in which you sleep.

Also make sure that there is no junk under your bed. Your house should be airy and well-lit. South-west and South-east are good directions for faster recovery and sound sleep helps to achieve peace of mind.

Take the right dose

Excess of everything is bad but the right dose could be a wonderful experience. Whether you are a teenager or a socialite, having too many late nights will culminate in stress and reduce your ability to enjoy life because the body loses its natural rhythm. Vaastu is not against late nights, (socialising) or eating out, it only recommends moderation and adds that excesses are committed when

Excess of everything is bad.

you have a blocked North-east or a higher wall towards North and East as compared to South or West. A lower floor level towards the West and South or more open space towards the South-west rather than North-east leads to self indulgence. When no sunlight comes into the house you deprive yourself of natural energy, and such a house creates negative rhythm and your mind remains disturbed. Yoga is highly recommended for such people.

Pranic healing cleans the aura

Can Vaastu help patients? Yes, but it also depends upon their doctors: do they want to make more money or do they want a faster recovery for their patients. If it is the former, then Vaastu is silent. The link between sickness and Vaastu is Ayurveda, where the primary concern is faster recovery of the patient. To expedite speedy recovery from sickness, Vaastu focuses on the South-east, the best direction for hospitals and nursing homes. The patient's head should be aligned towards the South or East and the negative *prana* being released by the patient should be negated by wiping the floor with a disinfectant and sea salt. Pranic healing also recommends taking a bath with a pinch of sea salt. Any conventional treatment must be supplemented with traditional prayers and holistic healing. Remember, a doctor treats but divinity cures.

The Vaastu cure for alcoholism

The reason for a person to turn to alcohol is usually the influence of bad company. Medically less heat in the body affects the pancreas that regulate the digestion of sugar by creating insulin. Due to excessive use of sugar, the pancreas start malfunctioning which leads to low blood pressure, migraines and at times creates more desire for

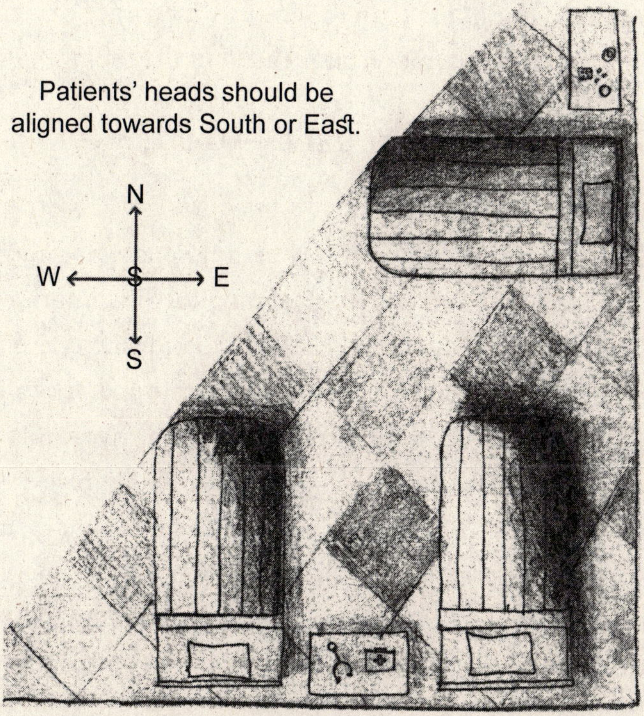

Vaastu can help in a speedy recovery.

RAKESH CHAWLA

sweet foods, leading to diabetes. Sometimes it even leads to alcoholism through hypoglycemia i.e. shortage of sugar when the gland is overactive. Vaastu says if your kitchen is towards the South-east the probability of achieving a solution is very high whereas if your kitchen happens to be along any other quadrant you need to supplement this element in your house by burning a candle towards the South east of your bedroom and your house. It is also suggested to sleep in a room towards the South-west corner of your house or in the South-west corner of your room. White colour is recommended in the room.

Energy follows thought—the Law of Miracles

The root cause of ill health is your emotional imbalance. It has been observed that we treat physical discomforts or diseases with medication, change in diet or lifestyle but refuse to change our mental equilibrium (mindset), thus ill health is bound to return. Directionally Vaastu puts a premium on South-west and South-east for fast recovery. It also emphasises positive thinking for better results as the fundamental principle for all esoteric concepts is 'Energy follows thought'. Therefore, whenever you follow Vaastu you definitely improve the energy levels of your premises and these energies or vibrations are channelised by your thought process. If you constantly think your situation is not improving, so it shall be. Energy will follow this thought. Whereas, if you keep a positive bent of mind, the results will be amazing. Remember, a smile adds to your face value and a positive thought improves your life. This *is* smart living.

Does Vaastu work faster on vegetarians?

There is no doubt that vegetarian food is easier to digest and is fast gaining popularity all over the world. Nevertheless, our *shastras* say *Jiva Jivasya Jivanam* which means life can only subsist on life. No matter what you eat, it has or once had *prana* or life. So, whether you enjoy and relish plant or animal protein, the argument against taking life is not restricted to vegetarianism. Do you know that many saints and sages did eat non-vegetarian food. Vaastu says you should eat whatever you can digest and if you are under a lot of external stress then you should not over-burden your internal system by wrong eating.

Heal Vaastu blocks with Reiki

Reiki transcends your physical, mental and emotional being, whereas Vaastu blocks are only objective or physical in nature. However, the relief with Reiki is confined to the span or duration of Reiki healing and the moment you stop giving Reiki, the negative effect of the block

Most commonly used enhancers.

will start causing discomfort once again. Therefore, it is advisable to circumvent the blockage with reorientation of furniture, fixing a mirror, a plant, lighting of a lamp or candle to improve the environment with positive vibrations and diffuse the negative energies of the block. To speed up the process, Reiki is an excellent catalyst. Any other form of healing also yields a beneficial outcome.

Chapter Ten

Children

Change the environment and your attitude

At work discipline is the order of the day whereas at home most parents find it hard to control their children. The factors that are responsible for this are television and insufficient time at the disposal of working parents coupled with pampering by grandparents. Things get out of hand when the children's bedroom happens to be located towards the South-west corner of the house. This being the zone of power, children realise they are all powerful and easily learn to manipulate and command their parents, while their attention span gets shorter and is reflected in the grades at school. Feeling guilty is not the answer. Shifting their bedroom will be appropriate and changing the environment of their existing room is essential.

Vaastu supplements karma

A very common concern of parents and children was expressed by one of my clients when he said, "My daughter has her board exams next month and she has three tutors coming in every day, yet she cannot concentrate. Can Vaastu be of any help?" Vaastu is a very strong support system that supplements your efforts (*karma)* with good fortune. If your room/ house is Vaastu perfect but you do not study (put in the re quired effort) will you pass with flying col ours? 'No'. Hard work is the key to success and it can be supplemented by studying in a room that is well lit, free of clutter, with the least amount of distractions - noise level should be negligible. One common practice of students while preparing for an important exam is to keep heaps of books on either side of their study table. Avoid this. It is also advised that early morn

Goddess Saraswati.

ing hours are excellent to grasp knowledge while evening hours are good for revision. Students are advised to face East or North while studying. Keeping an image in the room) of Goddess Saraswati is a boon. Placing a round-shaped crystal on the study table also helps. Include seven almonds in your diet and try to be a vegetarian for a month. With a light diet your energy is utilized for memorising rather than for digesting the food.

A large mirror helps build confidence in your child

Should children have a dressing table in their room? A small table with a large mirror above it is considered good as a full-length view of yourself in the morning and evening helps build confidence. A big table with a small mirror must be avoided. If the dressing table is on the side of the bed, it is considered auspicious, whereas if it is in front of the bed it brings bad luck. This alignment should be changed whenever possible, otherwise cover the mirror with a curtain before sleeping. When the dressing table is adjoining the study table it may become difficult to concentrate as the swing between looks and knowledge gets intensified and reaches its peak when the mirror is on the West wall. This causes kids to be more concerned about their impression on the opposite sex and concentration on the studies gets diluted. A mirror on the South wall can make the children very adamant and rebellious because of the extended zone of power.

Create the right atmosphere with love and affection

Over the years psychologists have attempted to define the elements in the home environment which are important for promoting intelligence and achievement. In the United States, a study called the Home Observation for Measurement of Environment (HOME) provided a systematic evaluation of the physical and social spheres of children's homes. It identified the following features of the home environment that affected child development in the initial years.

- How responsive are the parents to the child, both emotionally and verbally.
- The mother's acceptance of the child.
- The degree of discipline in the household—whether there were fixed times for daily tasks or not etc.
- Whether appropriate play material was available to the child.
- The variety in daily stimulation - changes in activities, opportunities to go to places, see new things, meet different people.

When one considers the atmosphere in which our children are being raised today, specially in the urban environment, the one factor that I rue most is lack of space. Children need physical space to run free, experience nature and expand their energies.

While most people are aware of how lack of adequate space can stunt the growth of a potted plant, few are willing to acknowledge that children could face a similar restriction when confined to closed spaces. It can actually impair their mental and emotional growth. Children who have no choice but to harbour the energy contained within could start showing signs of emotional distress, destructive streaks, etc.

The atmosphere you create for your growing children has a deep and long-lasting impact on their development. The nature or nurture debate could go on forever but the atmosphere in which we nurture our children can be infinitely adapted to suit the general requirements of each individual, each family, each specific need.

What is a good atmosphere? Our feelings are manifestations of elemental energies that we perceive as vibrations of a place. Everyone and everything emits vibrations. As per the quantum theory of physics, when matter is broken to a millionth part of its atom, it appears to be a vibration which conjugates as solids have a denser vibration than liquids or gases.

These subtle vibrations transcend our body through sensory perceptions and stimulate a reaction of like or dislike. If a place has a vibration in tandem with our body, we experience peace, otherwise it's a feeling of discomfort. Our mind is in harmony when the energy of our body and the place (house) are in resonance. This is what I call the right atmosphere. As per Feng Shui, it's Chi which creates an environment represented by Yin and Yang, negative and positive currents, similar to *Ida* and *Pingala* i.e. lunar and solar currents of Vaastu.

Hone the five universal elements with care and gentleness

To experience a good atmosphere of peace and harmony, we first need to consciously hone the universal elements of space, fire, water, earth and air.

Space: Native component: Sound. Sense organ : Ears.

Which is the most pleasing sound to the ears? The eternal "OM", "I love you", "You look good"—words of love and praise. More often than not we encounter just the opposite—heated arguments, running down one another, disgrace, disrespect.

If parents have had a tough day at work, why should the young ones suffer? As Sunil, a father of two decided: There was no point in screaming at the kids or his wife every evening because he was returning frustrated from work. Now when he parks his car in the garage, he sits for a couple of moments in silence, unwinds, thinks and pays attention to his thoughts of how blessed he is to have the love of his family to come home to. To add to the good influence, a wind chime in the centre of the house has been found to be useful.

Fire: Native component: Light. Sense organ : Eyes.

The colours surrounding a child, play on his psyche. Dark colours are depressing, tones of red cause irritability, pastel shades with a pleasing contrast have proved to be the best—green and blue for boys, lavender and lilac for girls. The rooms must be pleasantly bright, the visual perception must stimulate a pleasing sensation, any object which is not pleasing to the eye must be removed.

Water: Native component: Taste. Sense organ: Tongue.

Toddlers, especially, find themselves at the receiving end of a lot of attention as far as food is concerned. Since they are just learning to explore the gastronomic delights of the world, parents might be tempted to offer only those foods that the child shows a preference for. However, it is best not to encourage strong likes or dislikes for any one flavour, as each flavour is a unique combination of elements and serves a different purpose.

Do you see the elements of space missing in your child's diet? If you find any excesses in your child's diet please take corrective action right now because an elemental imbalance can result in physical discomfort.

Use the table below to examine your child's diet:

Flavour	***Elements***
Sweet	Earth and Water
Sour	Water and Fire
Salty	Earth and Fire
Bitter	Air and Space
Astringent	Air and Water
Pungent	Air and Fire

Earth: Native component: Smell. Sense organ—Nose.

Children should get maximum exposure to natural fragrances of flowers, herbs, plants, etc. rather than perfumes. It's a good idea to keep fresh flowers in your children's room. Potted plants are recommended inside the house. Make sure you use a mosquito repellent near a cluster of plants.

Air: Native component: Feelings. Sense organ—Skin.

A strong stimulus for a sense of belonging and love is a warm hug. The reaction normally is a big smile. Do you hug your child at least once a day if not more often? (Don't forget your spouse.)

Develop a routine of hugging your child as soon as he wakes up and when you tuck him into bed at night. This should become a spontaneous gesture of loving that accompanies your greeting. Children are very sensitive to vibrations and as they are in the process of discovering themselves. All elements play a very important role as this forms a benchmark on the basis of which inference takes place. The ability to infer is referred to as the intellect. Science will soon discover the equation between a good atmosphere and a bright intellect.

Examine your own home atmosphere and perhaps you will find new ideas emerging that will help you to reorganise the household in such a way that your children get the best out of you.

Chapter Eleven

Harmony

Prevent frequent friction for a harmonious relationship

Electricity follows the path of least resistance. Since all human beings have electrical currents in their body, it could be the reason why we also follow the path of least resistance. To some a fight or struggle comes naturally whereas most shy away or avoid confrontation of any sort. Friction is a necessary evil as nothing can move without it. Although friction is important, too much of it may become difficult to handle. When we experience too much friction it may be a good idea to investigate the amount of rust that has gathered on implements we use or in our surroundings. Get rid of it. Look into the activities towards the South-east quadrant (don't forget it's the zone

Bedroom on upper level.

of fire) of your house, factory or office and also take a look at your staircase (if there is one). If your bedroom is on the ground floor, it is preferred that the staircase ascends in a clockwise direction whereas if it is on the first floor then the staircase should descend in a clockwise direction. No step should ever be broken or chipped.

Litigation and false allegations are in the zone of fire

Can wrong Vaastu lead to false allegations? Yes, it can. The South east, the zone of fire, can bring a lot of fame when it is in harmony with the occupant. On the other hand, when it gets too violent it can cause loss of reputation, altercation and even litigation. If you have a water source towards the South/South east quadrant of your house or factory you are vulnerable to such a development or if your North-east is higher than the South-west and you face South-west while working, you may become a victim of false allegations. In a particular situation an export shipment got rejected on false charges. Vaastu recommends a change in direction of vision and suggests an uneven floor level to be made even with additional furniture or plants etc. At times putting additional weight towards the South-west helps a great deal.

Balance is vital

The law of balancing comes to the mid point or central axis. This also holds good for Vaastu because when the main directions are parallel to the house the balancing act is much simpler. However, when East, West, North,

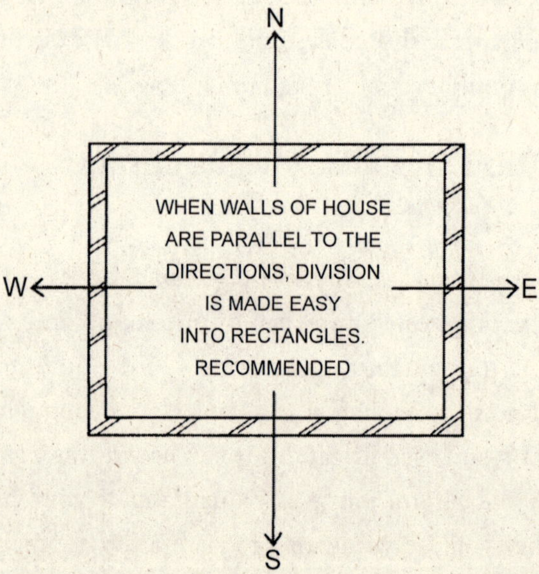

The balancing act.

South point towards the cor ners, things get compli cated. You know why?

In the former when you divide the house along the length and width you get four rectangles, which are referred to as quad rants, each housing its own element, whereas in the latter when you divide the house along the diagonal, each quadrant be comes a triangle which symbolises fire, so, irritability results from constant friction amongst the family members. To cir cumvent this deficiency, water and fire play an important role and both need to be harnessed. The centre of the house or the flat should also be left vacant. Avoid keeping any heavy object here. If there is a column in the centre, please do not panic, just wrap it with mirrors or hang a pair of flutes facing East.

Improve relationships between family members

When father and son are at loggerheads, tension is bound to rise. Similarly whenever there is rift between any two members of a family please check if the water source is in the South-east. Check whether the electrical cable is running across the house or in front of it. In one case—a villa in Gurgaon had 12 L.T. (low tension) cables and 1 H.T. (high tension) cable running below the ground level. Obviously there was tension in the family that led to separation. In such a case re-laying of the cable outside the boundary is the best solution. The ground should also be impregnated with lime powder. Another major cause of tension is when the bedroom is directly above or below a kitchen. Changing the room would be advisable or make sure the bed is not directly above the burner. If you have too much cactus on the balconies or near the front door it may be adding fuel to the fire. Remove it.

Perform *shanti paath* for peace and prosperity

When the relationship between your spouse and your parents becomes bitter, what can you do? Walking out of the situation is not easy and being constantly pulled in opposite directions is stressful. Vaastu suggests you look for sharp objects pointing towards your house or your bedrooms and remove them, and place fresh flowers or a small plant in the room. Next move the dustbin out of sight and remove all the cobwebs in your house.

SHANTI PAAT

If your bedroom is exactly above your parents' make sure the bed is not. Lighting a mustard oil lamp towards the South wall is extremely beneficial and finally if there is a door or a window towards the North-east please open it for good fortune to come in. Performing *Shanti paath* always brings peace. Do it twice a year.

Relocate rooms in order of seniority for benevolence

South-west is best for the head of the family.

When there are three or four members in a family of the same age group but different zodiac signs, which directions should be followed? In the good old days the head of the family was the only earning member so the main door was located as per his favourable direction and his bedroom was towards the South-west. Now, when there are three or four earning members un der different zodiac signs, the issue gets a little complicated. Vaastu recommends the eldest member, whether earning or not, should be housed towards the South-west, the younger ones should be in South-east and North-west respectively. In some houses it is observed that the highest earning member places himself in the South-west and the eldest gets pushed towards the North or East. Not only does it result in unpleas antness, there is complete mistrust and bitterness in such homes. In order to restore harmony, relocating the bedrooms in order of seniority is strongly recommended.

The centre of the house can jar communications

With the explosion of the internet, the world has shrunk to a global village. Communication has become fast and easy. While global communication is on the increase, in-house communication seems to be reducing day by day as one hardly gets time to talk to one another, leading to greater loneliness. Your efforts to communicate get a lot easier when you synchronize the tongue and ears. For that we need to look at the centre of the house or the zone of space which is the embodiment of sound. Try and avoid having a column or a wall or placing any heavy object in the *bhramasthana* or the exact centre of the house, as it tends to dislodge communication amongst the occupants.

If you discover there is a wall/column at the centre immediately place a mirror on it. In case of a heavy object, move it towards the South-west quadrant of the room/house. Hanging a bronze bell or a metal wind chime near the centre proves to be beneficial. Remove the television set from your bedroom. It is like taking out a splinter from your foot - painful to begin with, but healing in the long run.

Follow the law of tithing to prosper forever

Bite as much as you can chew. With a bigger bite you tend to gulp your food, causing indigestion. It is recommended to chew food 32 times before swallowing it. The same applies to your appetite for money where everyone wants bigger and bigger bites and some even want to chew on their neighbours' share. Indigestion is bound to occur, which eventually culminates in ill health, nervous breakdown, tensions, division in business or family. You must learn to chew. For those with a big appetite, Vaastu recommends the Law of Tithing which expands on the virtue of sharing. The law simply states—give one tenth of your income for a humanitarian cause and your income shall forever increase. The most prosperous community in the world are the Jews and it is believed they follow this law. In India amongst others, the Sikhs follow the same to a large extent (for their Gurdwaras) along with Kar Seva.

A crossroad leads to unpleasantness

When you are at a crossroad in life, it is always painful to choose the path to follow. If your house happens to be facing a crossroad, life could also be unpleasant. A corner house fetches a premium in the market if it has two or three sides open, but if it is at a dead end the householders could be miserable. Things become worse when the road comes straight into your main gate. In Vaastu this is referred to as *Veedhi Shool* and is capable of piercing your life. It is best to reflect back the energy by using a mirror or screening off the entrance with plants. Similarly, when your house is at a T-junction it could be translated into trouble in most areas of your life specially when the junction is towards the South-east and a depression in the West or vice versa always results in sour relationships. Amongst other remedial measures the placing of a pair of Ganeshas, (one in metal and the other wooden) does bring relief.

Change gears while driving

The way you drive your car is how you drive yourself in life. While driving we engage from low to high gears with increasing speed and if the speed-gear ratio is not maintained, the drive becomes rough and bumpy.

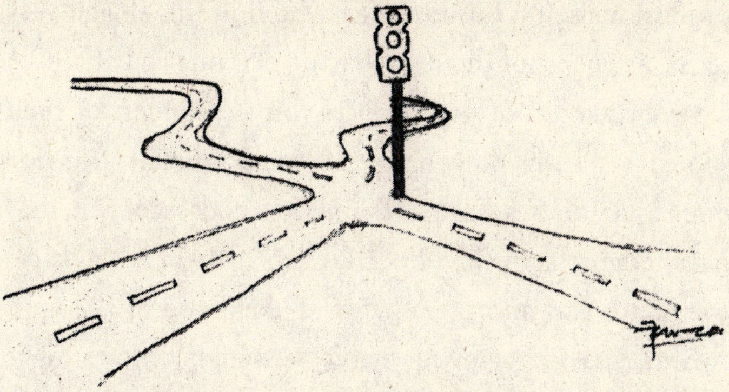

Choose the right path.

In life we need to change gears just as smoothly as we do in our vehicle. The changing of gears in life means understanding and accepting situations and increasing or reducing the pace of life accordingly. Very often we are adamant about our views and ignore the opinions and feelings of others around us. It's like refusing to change gears on a congested road.

When you feel your life's journey is becoming unpleasant make sure your bed does not have doors on either side, or you do not sleep or work under a beam or your bedroom is not above the kitchen as it would be similar to driving over a number of speed breakers!

T-shaped abodes can cause adultery!

The advertisement of a famous soft drink says, *"Yeh Dil Mange Mor*e." Today, one comes across a lot of middle aged professionals and businessmen who find this slogan very sensuous. Most of them are having extramarital affairs. A close evaluation of their houses (on the request of their spouses) reveals they have two predominant features; one, their houses have a T-junction and secondly, they have a depression (low floor levels). If these are towards the South-east and the West, the likelihood of the male member having a roving eye is very high. Interestingly, when this configuration is reversed you have an elevation instead of a depression - then the adultery effect shifts to the female member. Vaastu recommends levelling of the ground.

Have a Vaastu friendly house

Can bad Vaastu lead to a divorce or separation? Very often it is observed that divorce or separation takes place when the compatibility or tolerance level is low in either one or both the partners. These attributes develop when the thought processes are on different tangents. This usually occurs because the two have been brought up with different family values. When spouses with different value systems come together the merger is harmonious and balanced if the North-east of the house is open or at a lower level as compared to the rest of the house. The clash of value systems very often occurs when the North east is blocked off, say by a water cooler or has a wall or

T-shaped abodes can cause adultery in the family.

a toilet. Vaastu says the North-east of any house reflects the mindset of Vaastu *purusha* or manifest energy in that dwelling and when the same gets blocked, the chances of clashes in ideology are extremely high. Should this get coupled with a secondary defect, the manifestation of discord is even faster. Therefore, before filing for a divorce check the Vaastu friendliness of your house.

The North-west zone is also considered an ideal place to locate the bedroom of a newly married couple. A North-east bedroom should be avoided by young couples as it tends to create difficulties for conception or during pregnancy.

It is suggested that unmarried girls have their bedroom in the North-west corner of the house or it may even be used as a guest-room.

Chapter Twelve

Yoga and Meditation

Vaastu and yoga for dynamic living

Yoga is the union of body with mind. It synchronises thought, speech and action. Regular practice and deter mination help in our endeavour to have a supple body and a peaceful mind through various yogic kriyas. Vaastu also plays an important role in the practice of yoga specially in today's world where everyone is in the rat race (working for money). If

Look within.

you really want, you can make money work for you. To achieve this, all you need to do is to align your thought, speech and action. It helps to have a physical alignment or a straight axis running across the North-east (direction of thought), centre (di rection of speech) and South-west (direction for action). A regu lar, even-shaped North-east and South-west is good, and when either of them is cut off it tends to create problems. Avoid hav ing toilets in these two corners, and the South-west should be marginally higher than the North-east.

A prayer room in the North-east with feelings in your heart

What is the difference between prayers and meditation? When you pray you reach out to God establishing an external link whereas when you meditate you go within and establish an internal link. When Vaastu speaks of a place of worship, it refers to a prayer room because you can meditate anywhere anytime. It is good to have a common prayer room in the house as having independent ones in each bedroom creates a rift in the family. If you have a puja corner in your kitchen then make sure utensils are washed outside and you must wash your hands and feet before entering the kitchen. Try and avoid having a prayer corner in your bedroom. It's very auspicious to place an image of your God or deity towards the North-east of your house.

Ideally a prayer room should be in your heart but a prayer room at home can have many images of gods, goddesses and deities.

In a mandir, the place where the deity rests is called the sanctum sanctorum (G*arbh griha)*, the location of which is determined by the Vaastu grid and the installation ceremony is called *prana pratistha.* Once installed, the deity is considered to be a living being and is worshipped by everyone. According to Vaastu: East has Indra, South-east has Agni, South has Yama, South-west has Niruthi, West has Varun, North-west has Vayu, North has Kuber and North-east has Ishan (Shiva) while the centre point is *Brahma Bindu.* These are the nine directions, which also find a reference in numerology, the difference being they correspond to a direction instead of the deity. Vaastu strongly recommends you appease the deity whenever you confront a problem emerging from its direction. In Vaastu, each direction corresponds to a deity but in numerology, a number corresponds to a direction.

Keep a lotus in your prayer room as symbol of purity

Spring is the season for all plants and flowers to blossom, which is a visual treat to the eyes and is also a natural subduing factor for the violent fire element. Most flowers are hybrids except for the lotus which holds so much importance in any form of worship because it signifies purity. Lord Brahma is seated on a lotus. Goddess Laxmi is holding a lotus. So much so the symbol of a political party is also a lotus! In Tantra meditation the ascension of *kundalini* (dormant coiled energy) through various *chakras* or psychic centres is practiced. Each *chakra* is represented by a lotus with a different number of petals and assigned different colours. The *Mooladhara chakra* has 4 petals, S*wadhisthana chakra* has 6, *Manipura chakra* has 10, *Anahata chakra* has 16, V*ishuddhi chakra* has 32, A*jna Chakra* has 2 and S*ahasrara chakra* has a 1000. As the dormant energy ascends through these centres it opens up the petals. By removing the blocks of desires contained in each *chakra* it ultimately liberates the human being from the realm of desires attaining a state of *tatvatita,* that which is above the elements, and prepares for the ultimate union. Thus, Vaastu recommends keeping of a lotus in your prayer room to remind you to rise above your dreams.

Vaastu and Feng Shui

What is the similarity between Vaastu and Feng Shui? They are similar in most ways except their origin. Vaastu emerged at the apex of social hierarchy with the kings while Feng Shui was practised by the farmers. The literal translation of Feng Shui is 'wind water and both elements are of prime importance for crops. Feng Shui enjoys popularity in the West. According to some magazines even world leaders like Bill Clinton, Tony Blair and Amitabh Bachchan believe in it. Vaastu is fast catching up on lost ground as our politicians, MNCs and corporate houses have started taking an interest in this subject. A lot of NRIs refuse to move residence without seeking professional Vaastu advice. They feel no western concept teaches equanimity or peace of mind as our *Gita, Gayatri Mantra* and Ganga*jal.* The essence of all the three is found in Vaastu.

Vaastu meditation

What is Vaastu meditation? As you all know our universe comprises five basic elements in different ratios and each element is assigned a specific direction – a quadrant. Similarly our body also has psychic centres called *chakras* representing these elements—*Mooladhara* is earth, S*wadhisthana* is water, *Manipura* is fire, *Anahata* is air and *Vishuddhi* is space. A*jna* and S*ahasrara* belong to the realm of mind and spirit. Vaastu principles promote an alignment of a physical structure with the cosmos. And meditation helps to regulate the flow of energy inside your body through the *chakras* and *nadis* for perfect harmony between your body, mind and the environment. Regular practice of Vaastu meditation coupled with the chanting of *Gayatri Mantra* creates abundance through quantum vibrations in your surroundings. Sprinkling Ganga*jal* around your house helps to retain these vibrations for longer durations.

A modern truism is that the only thing constant in our fast paced life is change. Change can only happen in relation to a constant. For traffic to flow the road is constant, for the river to flow the river-bed is constant and for life to flow there has to be a constant. Modern thought says it is the 'constant supply of money' and ancient wisdom says it is the search of the soul. Both are correct and we must learn to integrate the two. Our inner journey is an ongoing process for which we must meditate and contemplate. Favourable directions are East or North and a good time to meditate is sunrise or sunset. For ten minutes in a day focus on your breath and count the number of times you inhale/exhale.

The traditional school of Vaastu being practiced today, which recommends following the *shastras* to the letter, is not only rigid but focuses on the structural aspect while neglecting the disciplinary aspect, a must for getting the desired results. Vaastu says in waking consciousness, the perception is through your sense organs. Whereas when you are asleep, your sense organs are detached from the mind but you have a direct perception in the dream state, making it impossible to distinguish between dream and reality. It is only when you wake up that you realise you were dreaming. Now the reality of the waking state is real and the reality in your dream state is also real. Since there cannot be two realities, then which one is real? Guru Nanakji in the *Japji Sahib* explains that this world is (half truth) and you can only discover the other half in meditation on obtaining a state of *turiya* or altered state of consciousness where you transcend waking consciousness and sleep consciousness simultaneously. The ideal time for practice is early morning. (Listen to the guided Vaastu Meditation audio cassette produced by FULL CIRCLE *PUBLISHING* Pvt. Ltd.)

Visit the *dhams* for salvation

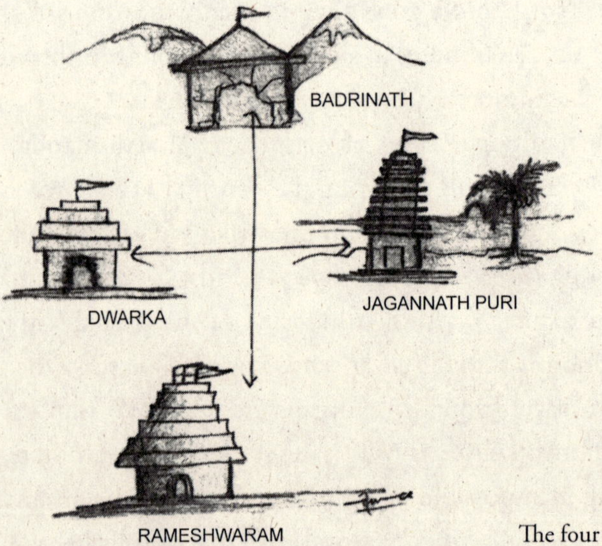

The four *dhams*.

A lot of people plan a pilgrimage to Vaishno Devi or Amarnath, some even venture out to Mansarovar Lake. Amongst all the holy places Vaastu mentions the four *dhams* (place of Gods) which are Puri (East), Rameshwaram (South), Dwarka (West) and Badrinath (North). It says a person must visit all the four *dhams* before the completion of his life's journey. You may do it in a year or maybe in a lifetime. All the four *dhams* are built in accordance to Vaastu. The vibrations are pure and extremely intense. The history of these temples goes back to over 5000 years, which reconfirms that Vaastu is not an overnight sen sation but a time-tested phenomenon. The final yatra of the *dhams* culminates at Pushkar, the only temple where Lord Brahma is worshipped.

Chapter Thirteen

Myths and Superstitions

Vaastu shastra

Vaastu shastra is an integral part of Vedic culture and philosophy. And the Vedas say that the five elements of nature, namely: earth (stability); water (purity); fire (energy and power); air (pervasiveness) and space (creativity and dynamism) are co-related with everything that goes on in the universe.

All the directions are natural

What are the ill effects of a South-west facing house? First of all you must understand that all the directions are only in reference to a concept. From the Vaastu point of view, the East and North represent inspiration and progress, South and West represent power and strength which is why the master bedroom or CEO's office are located in this corner. If South and West were not good at all Vaastu would never recommend the head of the family or of any organisation to be placed in this corner. In these directions the intensity of the sun's rays is more and carries a high content of infra red and ultra violet rays, hence we need protection from them in the form of a screen. In fact, in Europe and the USA business houses and entertainment companies that face the South-west have done extremely well. We do not have cosmic directions or universal directions. Can any branch of science tell us which direction of the cosmos our earth is in?

You may have noticed that when a black cat crosses the road people wait for someone else to cross before them. Think of the people who keep pets at home. Do they just sit still all day? More often than not we get carried away by myths and superstitions. You may also have heard that according to Vaastu, East is the direction of inspiration, North of wealth, West is the direction of the setting sun which is equated with retirement and South is said to be the direction of Yama, the god of death. I have met a lot of people who have been advised to shift their entrance from the South to North, some have even changed or shifted or moved residence while others have brought down their entire building just because it was facing South! I ask such advisers—if the South denotes death, does any direction offer immortality? I think such advice is irrational, baseless and impractical. If South and West are taboo then why is the master bedroom or CEO's office ideally recommended for the South-west corner? All directions are natural. We must know how to use them so that we are in NEWS (North-East West-South). That is, in the good books of nature.

A jinxed house

Can there be a house which is jinxed? Our *shastra*s do not speak of the devil or evil spirit but explain the accumulation of negative currents in some houses where a particular effect manifests itself irrespective of the occupant and every successive occupant experiences it, in the spheres of work, relationship or health. Such houses are referred to as jinxed, and it could be due to a particular Vaastu defect, which can be corrected to remove the

A jinxed house.

stigma attached to the property. It is rare to come across houses where inexplicable phenomena take place and the presence of discarnate energy form is experienced. Seeking professional help is advised and till such time as the problem is addressed, burning of camphor plus a mustard oil lamp is strongly recommended to help transmute the energy from discarnate to incarnate form.

Chapter Fourteen

Attitudes, Karma and Positivity

A face mask wards off jealousy

Whenever you are climbing the ladder of success you will always encounter certain elements of jealousy among your friends, colleagues and relatives. This phenomenon is a side-effect of gravitational force, which pulls everything down to earth. It is literally manifested in those around you who are trying hard to pull you down or discourage you because of jealousy. Vaastu says, accept it as a fact of life and you can circumvent its negative effect by mounting an ugly face mask above the main door or a string of 7 green chillies with a lemon in between and a piece of coal at the bottom. The effect gets magnified when the colour of the string is black.

Act with full awareness, it's like meditation

The evolution of mind and matter is easy to understand as the reference comes in many texts and forms but the evolution of life is a process which finds a reference only in the *Vedanta.* It examines a four-stage process of life which expands on the matrix of Consciousness-Perception-Sensation-Reaction. All living beings follow this evolutionary process. We become conscious of something when it is perceived through our sense organs. This stimulates a sensation (sometimes based on memory) followed by a reaction, which occurs spontaneously, a fraction of a second later, as it originates from the subconsciousness. Clearly, we live our lives more in the subconscious than the conscious mind. Vaastu helps us to become aware of this so that we live our lives meaningfully. It also states that instead of a subconscious reaction we should react with full awareness by making ourselves responsible for all our actions.

First achieve your goals in your mind

Whenever there is fire it shall radiate heat and give light. You cannot separate heat and light from fire as they are the inherent characteristics of this element. You find the same analogy in the soul, the intellect and the mind—the three are interwoven in divinity. The *Kathopanishad* says the *atman* or soul is perched on the chariot (the body), the *buddhi* (intellect) is the charioteer and the *mann* (mind) is the rein. The *indriyas* (sense organs) are the horses, which gallop on the path of sensual gratification which in Vaastu is referred to as *vaasanas*. The intellect with the help of the mind is required to exercise firm control over the senses, clamouring like a rider pulling the reins to control the horses while steering the chariot towards the path of *vaastava* (reality). It is the balancing of *vaasanas* with *vaastava* that forms the subject matter of Vaastu which is routed through the directions. The element which sheds light is fire and must be kindled by a burning desire and a strong will to achieve success which is described as progressive realisation of worthy goals. The most supporting direction is South-west.

As you sow, so shall you reap!

If you sow tomatoes can you expect apples to grow? But, very often we sow the seeds of selfishness and expect trust and loyalty to grow. When disappointed, we blame the environment or modern values. It is like saying the apples did not grow because the soil was not fertile. Once you understand this fundamental principle, things will start moving towards harmony.

According to Vaastu, a blocked or elevated North-east or a depressed South-east and North-west prevent us from being righteous and honest. Levelling out the land or filling up a depression, if there is one in the building or plot on which you live, would be ideal but may not be practical. In such a situation you can, notionally, raise the South-west by installing a flag pole and the depressed areas should be lit throughout the night.

Adding spices or a delicate topping to half cooked food serves no real purpose, similarly following Vaastu half-heartedly or with half cooked knowledge yields no outcome.

Do your karma to the best of your ability

Is poor Vaastu the only reason for our current problems? Ancient wisdom says we are only a projection of consciousness through the filters of our karma. This means our current life situation is due to our past deeds, which is reflected through Vaastu defects and planetary configurations. Also called our karmic map. We cannot

Take action!

RAKESH CHAWLA

undo our past but that should not prevent us from cleaning the filters by adopting remedial measures as recommended either at the beginning of any construction or through reorientation at a later stage. Not taking any action is a sin because you believe in destiny and you forego your karma to take corrective action. If you get a headache do you wait for it to go (destiny) or do you take medication? Vedic sciences offer a lot of medication for any discomfort in life in the form of yoga, meditation, breathing, Vaastu or spiritual healing and so on.

Enjoy your present, it is a gift from God

Some learned person said: The past is history, the future is a mystery and this moment is God's gift that is why we call it the 'present'. Unfortunately, few have learnt to enjoy this gift as the mind constantly oscillates between the past and the future. When the thought stimulating this oscillation is pleasant you become vibrant but when FUD (Fear, Uncertainty, Doubt) sets in, you become tense. Although it is not easy to stop this oscillation, it can be regulated and to ensure the same, have an even floor level in your house, office, shop and factory. When there is a depression towards the North or the East, the oscillation generates positive vibrations. When a depression is along the North-west, fear sets in, along the South-east, leads to uncertainty, and in the South-west makes you doubtful. Lighting a lamp and placing of mirrors in these corners prove to be beneficial.

Change your mindset to be successful

Why do Vaastu consultants offer varying suggestions? Even in subjects like self realisation or enlightenment different masters take different paths to reach the same destination. Similarly, in Vaastu there are different texts which may be broadly divided into the traditional or conventional and the modern school of thought. While the former follows the scriptures to the letter, the latter offers practical solutions to various issues. Both are equally effective. The diagnosis of a given problem shall always vary from person to person be it due to a Vaastu defect or a physical disease. Medical colleges impart the same knowledge to all the students yet on becoming doctors their opinions vary from one to another. On the other hand Vaastu is a subject that one learns through *diksha*—initiation by a guru along with dedication and experience. There is no formal education available on this subject, hence the opinion of consultants is bound to be different. There is no profession which follows a uniform school of thought, so how can Vaastu?

One thing I would like to make very clear to all the readers is that Vaastu or any other subject does not change our destiny. We as human beings can so divide our existence into three parts in which one third is our past karma, one third is our mind or will power and the balance one third is the influence of Vaastu. It is equally important to change our mindset (attitude) along with changing our surroundings to gain the maximum benefit from this subject. Only changing the environment with no change in the mindset is of little use. Your past karmas cannot be undone, therefore, what's destined shall happen but the way it happens or the intensity of the event can be diluted. For example, if it is forecast to rain we cannot prevent the rainfall but Vaastu can offer us an umbrella so that we don't get wet.

Conclusion

The time taken for the positive effects of Vaastu to manifest varies from person to person and largely depends on the problem for which guidance is sought.

The reader is thus advised to read this book with an open mind to enlighten himself on the subject.

About the Author

Raakesh Chawla is a renowned and respected Vaastu Consultant. He has worked with many homes, residential, business, commercial and industrial properties and successfully resolved many problems through Vaastu.

It was during his tenure with Philips India in 1988 that he was introduced to Vaastu Shastra. Since the past 15 years he has been refining and redefining the subject to make it easy to follow. His exhaustive research on Vaastu has found expression in *The Pocket Book of Vaastu,* published by FULL CIRCLE, in English and Hindi. The book has been reviewed by leading newspapers and magazines and has found a place in the New Age Top 10 bestsellers' lists. The book is a first of its kind in which the principles of Vaastu have been explained in extremely practical terms and simple language, with self evaluation exercises, thus giving the reader an exact understanding of the subject.

During the course of his intensive research on the subject Raakesh discovered the Energy Cycle, a combination of Vaastu Shastra, Feng Shui and Pyramidology which is being used in India and abroad with positive results.

He strongly believes that structural changes in any existing building is equivalent to surgery on the human body and one should undertake the same only as a last resort and that too when the discomfort experienced becomes unbearable. Mostly people are satisfied by simple reorientation of objects or by placing special mirrors, plants, etc.

Raakesh's current clientele spreads over a wide spectrum, ranging from politicians to MNC's. He has featured in various television programmes on Zee TV, ABN, DD Metro, BBC, Sony TV and Star Plus.

He believes this valuable science should not be confined to the scriptures or to the realm of a learned few, hence he has initiated the Institute of Vaastu Kala offering various courses in Vaastu Vidya. He regularly writes for various courses in Vaastu magazines and newspapers. His second book *Vaastu for Health, Wealth and Happiness* is focused around the queries he received during the past three years.

Raakesh Chawla
Institute of Vaastu Kala
H-91, Connaught Place, New Delhi-110001
Tel: 23320972, 23320947 E-mail: vaastukala@hotmail.com
web: www.vaastuwisdom.com